CLA

MYSTERIES

A Collection of Mind-bending Masterpieces

Edited by Molly Cooper
Illustrated by Barbara Kiwak

BARNES
&NOBLE
BOOKS
NEW YORK

ISBN: 0-7607-0608-5

Library of Congress Catalog Card Number: 96-140

Publisher: Jack Artenstein
General Manager, Juvenile Division: Elizabeth Amos
Director of Publishing Services: Rena Copperman
Editor-in-Chief, Juvenile Division: Barbara Schoichet
Managing Editor, Juvenile Division: Lindsey Hay
Art Director: Lisa-Theresa Lenthall
Design and Typesetting: Cheryl Carrington

Lowell House books can be purchased at special discounts when ordered in bulk for pre-
miums and special sales. Contact Department JH at the following address:
Lowell House Juvenile
2029 Century Park East, Suite 3290
Los Angeles, CA 90067

Manufactured in the United States of America

10 9 8 7 6 5 4 3 2 1

CONTENTS

Introduction
5

The Adventure of the Veiled Lodger
by Sir Arthur Conan Doyle
7

The Safety Match
by Anton Chekhov
22

The Stir Outside the Café Royal
A Story of Miss Van Snoop, Detective
by Clarence Rook
38

The Ruby and the Caldron
by Anna Katharine Green
47

A Curious Experience
by Mark Twain
81

The Oblong Box
by Edgar Allen Poe
111

CLASSIC MYSTERIES
Introduction

Dear Reader:

What is it about a mystery that captivates readers both young and old? Is it that we like to follow the trail of mastermind detectives and imagine how we ourselves might solve the case? Or is it the satisfaction we get by seeing criminals brought to justice? Maybe we just can't stand to be left in the dark and want a solution to every riddle.

Whatever the reason, there's no doubt that any story that combines elusive criminals and super sleuths is bound to find its way into any inquisitive reader's heart. To that end, the classic culprits and the crime-solvers who always catch their crooks in CLASSIC MYSTERIES are definitely worth investigating. They use ingenious deduction, incredible intuition, a little rule-bending, and quite often a dash of luck.

Eloquently written by such literary giants as Anton Chekhov, Mark Twain, and the creator of Sherlock Holmes himself, Sir Arthur Conan Doyle, many of the tales included in this timeless collection of mind-bending masterpieces are the forerunners of the mystery genre. In fact, several of the wonderful storytellers you're about to read have been dubbed the fathers and mothers of crime, and ensuing generations of mystery writers have modeled their plots and characters after the tricky twists these awesome authors weave into each of their spine-tingling tales.

So, are you ready to read about a dog whose bark leads to the solution of murder? Are you prepared to see what lies behind a woman's veil, and learn from her horribly scarred face how her husband met his shocking death? Then take out your magnifying glasses and fingerprint kits and enter the world of reason, intrigue, and imagination that follows. But be prepared for a challenge—these stories are liable to have you clueless . . . at least until you or some clever crime-solver figures them out.

THE ADVENTURE OF THE VEILED LODGER
by Sir Arthur Conan Doyle

Most people associate the name Arthur Conan Doyle with his brilliant character, Sherlock Holmes. But even though the world's most famous detective appears in four novels and fifty-six short stories, the charming criminal mastermind is only one of Doyle's many literary creations.

Born in Edinburgh, Scotland, in 1859, and educated at Stonyhurst and Edinburgh University, the writer-to-be first studied to be a doctor, and from 1882 to 1890 he did practice medicine. Fortunately for the literary world, however, Doyle's practice didn't completely occupy his time, and while waiting for patients, he began writing short stories. His early stories paid little, but his first Sherlock Holmes novel, A Study in Scarlet, *published in 1887, was a huge success. He then followed that publication with a historical novel,* Micah Clark, *published in 1888, which was also quite successful.*

During the Boer War, Doyle served as head physician in a field hospital in South Africa. Upon his return, he wrote a military history called The Great Boer War, *and a defense of British policy entitled* The Cause and Conduct of the War, *which was translated into many languages. It was for his military service that Doyle was knighted, and from 1902 on he was known as Sir Arthur Conan Doyle.*

In 1920, after several successful years of writing, the renowned author abandoned fiction in order to lecture on the possibilities of communicating with the spirits of those who had died. Doyle himself died in 1930, at the age of seventy-one, claiming that he and his wife had devised a code so that he could communicate with her after his passing.

Though his wife never got any communications from him, Doyle has managed to communicate to his readers through his legacy of short stories, all of which are full of intrigue and spine-tingling fun. And that surely holds true in "The Adventure of the Veiled Lodger," a tale narrated by Dr. John Watson, who eloquently describes how Scotland Yard's finest fictional detective, Sherlock Holmes, solved the mystery of a man's murder merely by reading the clues off a woman's scarred face.

One forenoon—it was late in 1896—I received a hurried note from Holmes asking for my attendance. When I arrived I found him seated in a smoke-laden atmosphere, with an elderly, motherly woman.

"This is Mrs. Merrilow, of South Brixton," said my friend with a wave of the hand. "Mrs. Merrilow does not object to tobacco, Watson, if you wish to indulge your filthy habits. Mrs. Merrilow has an interesting story to tell which may well lead to further developments in which your presence may be useful."

"Anything I can do—"

"You will understand, Mrs. Merrilow, that if I come to Mrs. Ronder I should prefer to have a witness. You will make her understand that before we arrive."

"Lord bless you, Mr. Holmes," said our visitor, "she is that anxious to see you that you might bring the whole parish at your heels!"

"Then we shall come early in the afternoon. Let us see that we have our facts correct before we start. If we go over them it will help Dr. Watson to understand the situation. You say that Mrs. Ronder has been your lodger for seven years and that you have only once seen her face."

"And I wish to God I had not!" said Mrs. Merrilow.

"It was, I understand, terribly mutilated."

"Well, Mr. Holmes, you would hardly say it was a face at all. That's how it looked. Our milkman got a glimpse of her once peeping out of the upper window, and he dropped his tin and the milk all over the front garden. That is the kind of face it is. When I was her—I happened on her unawares—she covered up quick, and then she said, 'Now, Mrs. Merrilow, you know at last why it is that I never raise my veil.'"

"Do you know anything about her history?"

"Nothing at all."

"Did she give references when she came?"

"No, but she gave hard cash, and plenty of it. A quarter's rent right down on the table in advance and no arguing about terms. In these times a poor woman like me can't afford to turn down a chance like that."

"Did she give any reason for choosing your house?"

"Mine stands well back from the road and is more private than most. Then again, I have no family of my own. I reckon she had tried others and found that mine suited her best. It's privacy she is after, and she is ready to pay for it."

"You say that she never showed her face from first to last save on the one accidental occasion? Well, it is a remarkable story, and I don't wonder that you want it examined."

"I don't, Mr. Holmes. I am quite satisfied so long as I get my rent. You could not have a quieter lodger, or one who gives less trouble."

"Then what has brought matters to a head?"

"Her health, Mr. Holmes. She seems to be wasting away. And there's something terrible on her mind. 'Murder!' she cries. 'Murder!' And once I heard her: 'You cruel beast! You monster!' she cried. It was in the night, and it fair rang through the house and sent shivers through me. So I went to her in the morning. 'Mrs. Ronder,' I says, 'if you have anything troubling your soul, there's the clergy,' I says, 'and there's the police. Between them you should get some help.'

"'For God's sake, not the police!' says she, 'and the clergy can't change what is past. And yet, it would ease my mind if someone knew the truth before I died.' 'Well,' says I, 'if you won't have the regulars, there is this detective we read about—beggin' your pardon, Mr. Holmes.

"And she, she fair jumped at it. 'That's the man,' says she. 'I wonder I never thought of it before. Bring him here, Mrs. Merrilow, and if he won't come, tell him I am the wife of Ronder's wild beast show. Say that, and give him the name Abbas Parva. That will bring him if he's the man I think he is.'"

"And it will, too," remarked Holmes. "Very good, Mrs. Merrilow. I should like to have a little chat with Dr. Watson. That will carry us till lunchtime. About three o'clock you may expect to see us in your house in Brixton."

Our visitor had no sooner waddled out of the room—no other verb can describe Mrs. Merrilow's method of progression—than Sherlock Holmes threw himself with fierce energy upon the pile of commonplace books in the corner. For a few minutes there was a constant swish of the leaves, and then with a grunt of satisfaction he came upon what he sought. So excited was he that he did not rise, but sat upon the floor like some strange Buddha, with crossed legs, the huge books all round him, and one open upon his knees.

"The case worried me at the time, Watson. Here are my marginal notes to prove it. I confess that I could make nothing of it. And yet I was convinced that the coroner was wrong. Have you no recollection of the Abbas Parva tragedy?"

"None, Holmes."

"And yet you were with me then. But certainly my own impression was very superficial. For there was nothing to go by, and none of the parties had engaged my services. Perhaps you would care to read the papers?"

"Could you not give me the points?"

"That is very easily done. It will probably come back to your memory as I talk. Ronder, of course, was a household word. He was the rival of Wombwell, and of Sanger, one of the greatest showmen of his day. There is evidence, however, that he took to drink, and that both he and his show were on the down grade at the time of the tragedy. The caravan had halted for the night at Abbas Parva, a small village in Berkshire, when this horror occurred. They were on their way to Wimbledon, and they were simply camping and not exhibiting, as the place is so small a one that it would not have paid them to open.

"They had among their exhibits a very fine North African lion. Sahara King was its name, and it was the habit, both of Ronder and his wife, to give exhibitions inside its cage. Here, you see, is a photograph of the performance by which you will perceive that Ronder was a huge porcine person and that his wife was a very magnificent woman. It was deposed at the inquest that there had been signs that the lion was dangerous, but, as usual, familiarity begat contempt, and no notice was taken of the fact.

"It was usual for either Ronder or his wife to feed the lion at night. Sometimes one went, sometimes both, but they never allowed anyone else to do it, for they believed that so long as they were the food-carriers he would regard them as benefactors and would never molest them. On this particular night, seven years ago, they both went, and a very terrible happening followed, the details of which have never been made clear.

"It seems that the whole camp was roused near midnight by the roars of the animal and the screams of the woman. The different grooms and employees rushed from their tents, carrying lanterns, and by their light an awful sight was revealed. Ronder lay, with the back of his head crushed in and deep claw-marks across his scalp, some ten yards from the cage, which was open. Close to the door of the cage lay Mrs. Ronder upon her back, with the creature squatting and snarling above her. It had torn her face in such a fashion that it was never thought that she could live. Several of the circus men, headed by Leonardo, the strong man, and Griggs, the clown, drove the creature off with poles, upon which it sprang back into the cage and was at once locked in.

"How it had got loose was a mystery. It was conjectured that the pair intended to enter the cage, but that when the door was loosed the creature bounded out upon them. There was no other point of interest in the evidence save that the woman in a delirium of agony kept screaming, 'Coward! Coward!' as she was carried back to the van in which they lived. It was six months before she was fit to give evidence, but the inquest was duly held, with the obvious verdict of death from misadventure."

"What alternative could be conceived?" said I.

"You may well say so. And yet there were one or two points which worried young Edmunds, of the Berkshire Constabulary. A smart lad! He was sent later to Allahabad.

That was how I came into the matter, for he dropped in and smoked a pipe or two over it."

"A thin, yellow-haired man?"

"Exactly. I was sure you would pick up the trail presently."

"But what worried him?"

"Well, we were both worried. It was so deucedly difficult to reconstruct the affair. Look at it from the lion's point of view. He is liberated. What does he do? He takes half a dozen bounds forward, which brings him to Ronder. Ronder turns to fly—the claw marks were on the back of his head—but the lion strikes him down. Then, instead of bounding on and escaping, he returns to the woman, who was close to the cage, and he knocks her over and chews her face up. Then, again, those cries of hers would seem to imply that her husband had in some way failed her. What could the poor devil have done to help her? You see the difficulty?"

"Quite."

"And then there was another thing. It comes back to me now as I think it over. There was some evidence that just at the time the lion roared and the woman screamed, a man began shouting in terror."

"This man Ronder, no doubt."

"Well, if his skull is smashed in you would hardly expect to hear from him again. There were at least two witnesses who spoke of the cries of a man mingled with those of a woman."

"I should think the whole camp was crying out by then. As to the other points, I think I could suggest a solution."

"I should be glad to consider it."

"The two were together, ten yards from the cage, when the lion got lose. The man turned and was struck down. The woman conceived the idea of getting into the cage and shutting the door. It was her only refuge. She made for it, and just as she reached it the beast bounded after her and knocked her over. She was angry with her husband for having encouraged the beast's rage by turning. If they had faced it they might have cowed it. Hence her cries of 'Coward!'"

"Brilliant, Watson! Only one flaw in your diamond."

"What is the flaw, Holmes?"

"If they were both ten paces from the cage, how came the beast to get loose?"

"Is it possible that they had some enemy who loosed it?"

"And why should it attack them savagely when it was in the habit of playing with them, and doing tricks with them inside the cage?"

"Possibly the same enemy had done something to enrage the lion."

Holmes looked thoughtful and remained in silence for some moments.

"Well, Watson, there is this to be said for your theory. Ronder was a man of many enemies. A huge bully of a man, he cursed and slashed at everyone who came in his way. I expect those cries about a monster, of which our visitor has spoken, were nocturnal reminiscences of the dear departed. However, our speculations are futile until we have all the facts. There is a partridge on the sideboard, Watson, and a bottle of Montrachet. Let us renew our energies before we make a fresh call upon them."

When our hansom deposited us at the house of Mrs. Merrilow, we found that plump lady blocking the door of her humble abode. It was clear that her chief preoccupation was lest she should lose a valuable lodger, and she implored us, before showing us up, to say and do nothing which could lead to so undesirable an end. Then, having reassured her, we followed her up the straight, badly carpeted staircase and were shown into the room of the mysterious lodger.

It was a musty, ill-ventilated place, as might be expected, since its inmate seldom left it. From keeping beasts in a cage, the woman seemed, by some retribution of fate, to have become herself a beast in a cage. She sat in a broken armchair in the shadowy corner of the room. Long years of inaction had coarsened her figure, but at some period it must have been beautiful, and was still full and voluptuous. A dark veil covered her face. It was cut off close at her upper lip and disclosed a perfectly shaped mouth and a delicately rounded chin. I could well conceive that she had indeed been a remarkable woman. Her voice, too, was well modulated and pleasing.

"My name is not unfamiliar to you, Mr. Holmes," said she. "I thought that it would bring you."

"That is so, madam, though I do not know how you are aware that I was interested in your case."

"I learned it when I had recovered my health and was examined by Mr. Edmunds, the county detective. I fear I lied to him. Perhaps it would have been wiser had I told the truth."

"It is usually wiser to tell the truth. But why did you lie?"

"Because the fate of someone else depended upon it. I know that he was a very worthless being, and yet I would not have his destruction upon my conscience. We had been so close—so close!"

"But has this impediment been removed?"

"Yes, sir. The person that I allude to is dead."

"Then why not now tell the police anything you know?"

"Because there is another person to be considered. That other person is myself. I could not stand the scandal which would come from a police examination. I have not long to live, but I wish to die undisturbed. And yet I wanted to find one man of judgment to whom I could tell my terrible story, so that when I am gone all might be understood."

"You compliment me, madam. At the same time, I am a responsible person. I do not promise you that when you have spoken I may not myself think it my duty to refer the case to the police."

"I think not, Mr. Holmes. I know your character and methods too well, for I have followed your work for some years. Reading is the only pleasure which fate has left me, and I miss little which passes in the world. But in any case, I will take my chance of the use which you may make of my tragedy. It will ease my mind to tell it."

"My friend and I would be glad to hear it."

The woman rose and took from a drawer the photograph of a man. He was a professional acrobat, a man of magnificent physique, with huge arms folded across his swollen chest and a smile breaking from under his heavy moustache—the self-satisfied smile of the man of many conquests.

"That is Leonardo," she said.

"Leonardo, the strong man, who gave evidence?"

"The same. And this—this is my husband."

It was a dreadful face—a human pig, or rather a human wild boar, for it was formidable in its bestiality. One could imagine that vile mouth champing and foaming in its rage, and one could conceive of those small, vicious eyes darting pure malignancy as they looked forth upon the world. Ruffian, bully, beast—it was all written on that heavy-jowled face.

"Those two pictures will help you, gentlemen, to understand the story. I was a poor circus girl brought up on sawdust, and doing springs through the hoop before I was ten. When I became a woman this man loved me, if such lust as his can be called love, and in an evil moment I became his wife. From that day I was in hell, and he was the devil who tormented me. There was no one in the show who did not know of his treatment. They all pitied me and they all loathed him, but what could they do? They feared him one and all. He was terrible at all times, and murderous when he was drunk. Again and again he was had up for assault, and for cruelty to the beasts, but he had plenty of money and the fines were nothing to him. The best men all left us, and the show began to go downhill. It was only Leonardo and I who kept it up—with little Jimmy Griggs, the clown. Poor devil, he had not much to be funny about, but he did what he could to hold things together.

"Then Leonardo came more and more into my life. You see what he was like. I know now the poor spirit that was hidden in that splendid body, but compared to my husband he seemed like the angel Gabriel. He pitied me and helped me, till at last our intimacy turned to love—deep, deep, passionate love, such love as I had dreamed of but never hoped to feel. My husband suspected it, but I think that he was a coward as well as a bully, and that Leonardo was the one man that he was afraid of. He took revenge in his own way by torturing me more than ever. One night my cries brought Leonardo to the door of our van. We were near tragedy that night, and soon my lover and I understood that it could not be avoided. My husband was not fit to live. We planned that he should die.

"Leonardo had a clever, scheming brain. It was he who planned it. I do not say that to blame him, for I was ready to go with him every inch of the way. But I should never have had the wit to think of such a plan. We made a club—Leonardo made it—and in the leaden head he fastened five long steel nails, the points outward, with just such a spread as the lion's paw. This was to give my husband his death-blow, and yet to leave the evidence that it was the lion which we would loose who had done the deed.

"It was a pitch-dark night when my husband and I went down, as was our custom, to feed the beast. We carried with us the raw meat in a zinc pail. Leonardo was waiting at the big van which we should have to pass before we reached the cage. He was too slow, and we walked past him before he could strike, but he followed us on tiptoe and I heard the crash as the club smashed my husband's skull. My heart leaped with joy at the sound. I sprang forward, and I undid the catch which held the door of the great lion's cage.

"And then the terrible thing happened. You may have heard how quick these creatures are to scent human blood, and how it excites them. Some strange instinct had told the creature in one instant that a human being had been slain. As I slipped the bars it bounded out and was on me in an instant. Leonardo could have saved me. If he had rushed forward and struck the beast with his club he might have cowed it. But the man lost his nerve. I heard him shout in his terror, and then I saw him turn and fly. At the same instant the teeth of the lion met in my face. Its hot, filthy breath had already poisoned me and I was hardly conscious of pain. With the palms of my hands I tried to push the great steaming, blood-stained jaws away from me, and I screamed for help. I was conscious that the camp was stirring, and then dimly I remembered a group of men. Leonardo, Griggs, and others, dragging me from under the creature's paws. That was my last memory, Mr. Holmes, for many a weary month. When I came to myself and saw myself in a mirror, I cursed that lion—not because he had torn away my beauty but because he had not torn away my life. I had but one desire, and I had enough money to gratify it. It was that I should cover myself so that my poor face should be seen by none, and that I should dwell where none I had ever known should find me. That was all that was left to me to do—and that is what I have done. A poor wounded beast that has crawled into its hole to die—that is the end of Eugenia Ronder."

We sat in silence for some time after the unhappy woman had told her story. Then Holmes stretched out his long arm and patted her hand with such a show of sympathy as I had seldom known him to exhibit.

"Poor girl!" he said. "The ways of fate are indeed hard to understand. If there is not some compensation hereafter, then the world is a cruel jest. But what of Leonardo?"

"I never saw him or heard from him again. Perhaps I have been wrong to feel so bitterly against him. He might as soon have loved one of the freaks we carried round the country as the thing which the lion had left. But a woman's love is not so easily set aside. He had left me under the beast's claws, he had deserted me in my need, and yet I could not bring myself to give him to the gallows. For myself, I cared nothing what became of me. What could be more dreadful than my actual life? But I stood between Leonardo and his fate."

"And he is dead?"

"He was drowned last month when bathing near Margate."

"And what did he do with his five-clawed club, which is the most singular and ingenious part of all your story?"

"I cannot tell, Mr. Holmes. There is a chalk-pit by the camp, with a deep green pool at the base of it. Perhaps in the depths of that pool—"

"Well, it is of little consequence now. The case is closed."

"Yes," said the woman, "the case is closed."

We had risen to go, but there was something in the woman's voice which arrested Holmes's attention. He turned swiftly upon her.

"Your life is not your own," he said. "Keep your hands off of it."

"What use is it to anyone?"

"How can you tell? The example of patient suffering is in itself the most precious of all lessons to an impatient world."

The woman's answer was a terrible one. She raised her veil and stepped forward into the light.

"I wonder if you would bear it," she said.

It was horrible. No words can describe the framework of a face when the face itself is gone. Two living and beautiful brown eyes looking sadly out from that grisly ruin did but make the view more awful. Holmes held up his hand in a gesture of pity and protest, and together we left the room.

Two days later, when I called upon my friend, he pointed with some pride to a small blue bottle upon his mantelpiece. I picked it up. There was a red poison label. A pleasant almondy odour rose when I opened it.

"Prussic acid?" said I. "Exactly. It came by post. 'I send you my temptation. I will follow your advice.' That was the message. I think, Watson, we can guess the name of the brave woman who sent it."

THE SAFETY MATCH

by Anton Chekhov

Born on January 17, 1860, in Taganrog, a small town in Russia, Anton Pavlovich Chekhov spent much of his unhappy childhood working at his father's unheated store late into the night. In 1876, when the business went bankrupt, Chekhov's father fled to Moscow to escape debtors' prison, and his mother took Chekhov's seven younger siblings and joined her husband. Chekhov, who was only sixteen at the time, was left behind to finish school and to be the family's main support through his tutoring.

After completing his schooling, Chekhov moved to Moscow to join his family. There he studied medicine and supported the family once again, now by publishing short stories. These stories, the first of which appeared in 1880 in Strekoza, a magazine whose name means "dragonfly," paid for Chekhov's medical school.

Graduating in 1884, Chekhov, like Sir Arthur Conan Doyle, became a doctor. But in 1885, after the young author/physician was encouraged by the novelist Dimitry Grigorovich, Chekhov began taking his writing more seriously. Dominated by the firm belief that unless he was improving man's lot his efforts were useless, Chekhov started to pen his dramatic works, most of which were infused with a social consciousness.

In 1889, however, his first full-length drama, The Wood Demon, was produced and was nearly a complete failure. But the year was tragic for Chekhov in other ways than professionally. Also in that *year the budding playwright lost his brother Nicolai to tuberculosis, a disease that would eventually kill him as well.*

Because of these setbacks, Chekhov decided to devote his life to philanthropic activities until 1896, when he was tempted by the theater again, only to produce another failure, The Seagull. After that Chekhov vowed never to write drama again, only to break this vow two years later by writing some of his most famous plays, including Uncle Vanya, Three Sisters, and The Cherry Orchard.

In 1898, the newly built Moscow Art Theater restaged The Seagull and made it a huge success, and it was at this theater that Chekhov also met the actress Olga Knipper, whom he married in 1901. Their happiness, however, was marred by the now famous playwright's increasing ill health, which he finally succumbed to on July 15, 1904.

Chekhov's short story "The Safety Match" is a delightful mystery that illustrates a lighter side to the author's traditionally heavier works. Although it involves a murder, the method in which the characters go about solving the crime and the surprise ending cannot help but leave an ironic smile on every reader's face.

I

On the morning of October 6, 1885, in the office of the Inspector of Police, appeared a respectably dressed man, who announced that his master, Marcus Ivanovitch Klausoff, a retired officer of the Horse Guards, had been murdered. While making this announcement the young man's hands trembled and his eyes were full of terror.

"Whom am I addressing?" asked the inspector.

"Psyekoff, Lieutenant Klausoff's agent; agriculture and engineering expert!"

The inspector and his deputy, on visiting the scene of the occurrence in company with Psyekoff, found the following: Near the wing in which Klausoff had lived was gathered a dense crowd. The news of the murder had sped as swift as lightning through the neighborhood, and the peasantry, thanks to its being a holiday, had hurried together from all the neighboring villages. There was much commotion. Here and there, pale, tear-stained faces were seen. The door of Klausoff's bedroom was found locked. The key was in the lock inside.

"It is quite clear that the scoundrels got in by the window!" said Psyekoff as they examined the door.

They went to the garden, into which the bedroom window opened. The window looked dark and ominous. It was covered by a faded green curtain. One corner of the curtain was slightly turned up, which made it possible to look into the bedroom.

"Did anyone look into the window?" asked the inspector.

"Certainly not, your worship!" answered Ephraim, the gardener, a little gray-haired old man. "Who's going to look in, if all their bones are shaking?"

"Ah, Marcus Ivanovitch, Marcus Ivanovitch!" sighed the inspector, looking at the window. "I told you you would come to a bad end! I told the dear man, but he wouldn't listen! Dissipation doesn't bring any good!"

"Thanks to Ephraim," said Psyekoff. "But for him, we would never have guessed. He comes to me this morning, and says, 'Why is the master so long getting up? He hasn't left his bedroom for a whole week!' The thought flashed through my mind that we haven't had a sight of him since last Saturday, and today is Sunday! Seven whole days—not a doubt of it!"

"Ay, poor fellow," again sighed the inspector. "He was a clever fellow, finely educated, and kind-hearted at that! But he was a waster, God rest his soul! I was prepared for anything since he refused to live with Olga Petrovna. Poor thing, a good wife, but a sharp tongue! Stephen!" the inspector called to one of his deputies. "Go over to my house this minute, and send Andrew to report to the police captain! Then go as fast as you can to the examining magistrate, Nicholas Yermolaiyevitch, and tell him to come over here."

Ten minutes later he was sitting on a stool, and sipping scalding tea. "There you are!" he was saying to Psyekoff. "A noble by birth, and what did he come to? He drank and dissipated and—there you are—he's murdered."

After a couple of hours the examining magistrate drove up. Nicholas Yermolaiyevitch Chubikoff—for that was his name —had been wrestling with the duties of his office for a quarter of a century. He was accompanied to the scene of the murder by his inveterate companion and assistant, Dukovski, a tall, young fellow of twenty-six.

"Is it possible, gentlemen?" cried Chubikoff, entering Psyekoff's room. "Marcus Ivanovitch? Murdered? No! It is impossible!"

"Go in there," sighed the inspector.

Going to the wing, the examining magistrate began his work by examining the bedroom door. Nothing was found which could serve as a clue. They had to break in the door. Then Chubikoff, his assistant, and the inspector hesitatingly, one after the other, entered the room, and their eyes met the following sight: Beside the single window stood a big wooden bed with a huge feather mattress. On the rumpled feather bed lay a crumpled quilt. On the table beside the bed lay a silver watch and a silver twenty-kopeck piece. Beside them lay some sulphur matches. Under the table lay one boot, covered with dust. Casting a glance around the room, the magistrate frowned and grew red in the face.

"Scoundrels!" he muttered, clenching his fists. Chubikoff went up to the window, pulled the curtain to one side, and carefully pushed the window. "It opens, you see! It wasn't fastened. Hm! There are tracks under the window. Somebody got in here. We must examine the window thoroughly."

"There is nothing special to be found on the floor," said Dukovski. "The only thing I found was a struck safety match. Here it is! So far as I remember, Marcus Ivanovitch did not smoke. And he always used sulphur matches, never safety matches. Perhaps this safety match may serve as a clue!"

"Oh, do shut up!" cried the magistrate deprecatingly. "Instead of chasing matches, you had better examine the bed!"

After an examination of the bed, Dukovski reported, "There are no spots, either of blood or anything else. On the pillow there are signs of teeth. The general appearance of the bed gives grounds for thinking that a struggle took place on it."

"I know there was a struggle without your telling me! Instead of looking for struggles, you had better—"

"Here is one boot, but there is no sign of the other. It proves that they strangled him while he was taking his boots off. He hadn't time to take the second boot off when—"

"And how do you know they strangled him?"

"There are marks of teeth on the pillow."

"Listen to his foolishness! Better come into the garden. You would be better employed examining the garden than digging around here."

When they reached the garden they began by examining the grass. The grass under the window was crushed and trampled. A bushy burdock growing under the window close to the wall was also trampled. On the upper branches were found some fine hairs of dark blue wool.

"What color was his last suit?" Dukovski asked Psyekoff.

"Yellow canvas."

"Excellent! You see they wore blue!"

At this point Police Captain Artsuybasheff Svistakovski and Dr. Tyutyeff arrived. The captain greeted them and immediately began to satisfy his curiosity.

The examination of the grass and the bushes nearest the window yielded a series of useful clues. For example, Dukovski succeeded in discovering a long, dark streak, made up of spots, on the grass, which led some distance into the center of the garden. The streak ended under one of the lilac bushes in a dark brown stain. Under this same lilac bush was found a boot, which turned out to be the fellow of the boot already found in the bedroom.

"That blood stain was made some time ago," said Dukovski.

"He wasn't strangled, if there was blood," said Chubikoff.

"They strangled him in the bedroom; and here, fearing he might come round again, they struck him a blow with some sharp-pointed instrument. The stain under the bush proves that he lay there a considerable time, while they were looking about for some way of carrying him out of the garden. The boot confirms my idea that they murdered him while he was taking his boots off before going to bed. He had already taken off one boot, and the other, this one here, he had only had time to take half off. The half-off boot came off by itself, while the body was being dragged, and fell—"

"There's a lively imagination for you!" laughed Chubikoff. "Instead of arguing and deducing, it would be much better if you took some of the bloodstained grass for analysis!"

When they had finished their examination, the investigators went to the director's office to write their report and have breakfast. While they were breakfasting they went on talking:

"The watch, the money, and so on—all untouched—" Chubikoff began, "show as clearly as two and two are four that the murder was not committed for the purpose of robbery."

"The murder was committed by an educated man!" insisted Dukovski. "The safety match proves that to me, for the peasants hereabouts are not yet acquainted with safety matches. Only the landowners use them, and by no means all of them. And it is evident that there was not one murderer, but at least three. Two held him, while one killed him. The murderers came on him while he was taking off his boots. If he was taking off his boots, that proves that he wasn't asleep!"

"Stop inventing your deductions! Better eat!"

"In my opinion," said the gardener Ephraim, "it was nobody but Nicholas who did this dirty trick."

"And who is Nicholas?"

"The master's valet," answered Ephraim. "He's a rascal, your worship! He always took the master his vodka and put the master to bed. And I also venture to point out to your worship, he once boasted at the public house that he would kill the master! It happened on account of Aquilina, the woman, you know. She pleased the master; the master made friends with her himself, and Nicholas—naturally, he was mad. He is rolling about drunk in the kitchen now, crying and telling lies, saying he is sorry for the master."

The examining magistrate ordered Nicholas to be brought. Nicholas, a lanky young fellow, entered Psyekoff's room, and bowed low before the magistrate. His face was sleepy and tear-stained.

"Where is your master?" Chubikoff asked him. "Where is his body?"

"They say he was dragged out of the window and buried in the garden!"

"Hmm . . . The results of the investigation are already known in the kitchen!—That's bad! Where were you, my good fellow, the night the master was murdered?"

"I don't know, your worship," he said. "I was drunk and don't remember."

"An alibi!" whispered Dukovski, rubbing his hands.

"And why is there blood under the master's window?"

"That blood doesn't amount to anything, your worship! I was cutting a chicken's throat. I was doing it quite simply, in the usual way, when all of a sudden it broke away and started to run. That is where the blood came from."

"Do you know Aquilina?"

"Yes, your worship, I know her."

"And the master cut you out with her?"

"Not at all. He cut me out—Mr. Psyekoff there, Ivan Mikhailovitch; and the master cut Ivan Mikhailovitch out. That is how it was."

Psyekoff grew confused and began to scratch his left eye. Dukovski noticed that the director had dark blue trousers, which he had not observed before. The dark blue trousers reminded him of the dark blue threads found on the burdock. Chubikoff in his turn glanced suspiciously at Psyekoff.

"Go!" he said to Nicholas. "And now permit me to put a question to you, Mr. Psyekoff. Of course you were here last Saturday evening?"

"Yes! I had supper with Marcus Ivanovitch about ten."

"And afterward?"

29

"Afterward—afterward—really, I do not remember," stammered Psyekoff. "I had a good deal to drink at supper. I don't remember when or where I went to sleep. Why are you all looking at me like that, as if I was the murderer?"

"Do not get agitated. Did you know Aquilina?"

"There's nothing extraordinary about that—"

"She first liked you and then preferred Klausoff?"

"Yes."

An oppressive silence began and lasted fully five minutes. It was finally broken by the examining magistrate. "We must go to the house and talk with Maria Ivanovna, the sister of the deceased. Perhaps she may be able to supply some clues."

They found Klausoff's sister, Maria Ivanovna, at prayer before a big case of family icons. When she saw the portfolios in her guests' hands, and their official caps, she grew pale.

"We have come to you with a request. Of course, you have heard already. There is a suspicion that your dear brother has been murdered. Could you not help us with some clue?"

"Oh, don't ask me!" said Maria Ivanovna, growing still paler, and covering her face with her hands. "I can tell you nothing. I beg you! I know nothing—Oh, no! no!—not a word about my brother! If I die, I won't say anything!"

Maria Ivanovna began to weep, and left the room. The investigators looked at each other, shrugged their shoulders, and beat a retreat.

"Confound the woman!" scolded Dukovski, going out of the house. "It is clear she knows something and is concealing it!"

In the evening Chubikoff and his deputy, lit on their road by the pale moon, wended their way homeward. At the end of their journey the deputy said, "It is quite certain that Nicholas had something to do with the matter. His alibi betrays him, body and bones. But it is also certain that he did not set the thing going. And the humble Psyekoff was not without some share in the matter. His dark blue trousers, his agitation, his alibi, and Aquilina—"

"So, according to you, whoever knew Aquilina is the murderer! You were one of Aquilina's admirers yourself—does it follow that you are implicated too?"

"Aquilina was cook in your house for a month. I am saying nothing about that! It isn't the woman that matters, old chap! It is the mean, nasty, low spirit of jealousy that matters. The retiring young man was not pleased when they got the better of him, you see! His vanity, don't you see? He wanted revenge. Then, those thick lips of his suggest passion. So there you have it: wounded ego and passion. That is quite enough motive for a murder. We have two of them in our hands; but who is the third?" Dukovski crammed his hat down over his eyes and pondered. He remained silent until the carriage rolled up to the magistrate's door. "Eureka!" he said, entering the little house and throwing off his overcoat. "The third person, who acted in concert with that scoundrel Psyekoff, and did the smothering, was a woman! Yes! I mean the murdered man's sister, Maria Ivanovna! How do you explain her unwillingness to give us any information? She detested her brother. She never forgave him for living apart from his wife. There is where the germ of her hate was hatched, she smothered him! O treacherous woman! My dear old man, won't you entrust this business to me? Friend, I began it and I will finish it!"

Chubikoff shook his head and frowned. "We know how to manage difficult matters ourselves," he said.

Dukovski flared up, banged the door, and disappeared.

"Clever rascal," muttered Chubikoff, glancing after him.

"Awfully clever! But too much of a hothead. I must buy him a cigar case at the fair as a present."

The next day a young man, who came from Klausoff's place, was introduced to the magistrate's office. He said he was the shepherd Daniel, and brought a very interesting piece of information. "I was a bit drunk," he said. "I was with my pal till midnight. On my way home I went into the river for a bath. I was taking a bath, when I looked up. Two men were walking along the dam, carrying something black. 'Shoo!' I cried at them. They got scared, and went off like the wind. Strike me dead, if they weren't carrying away the master!"

That same day, toward evening, Psyekoff and Nicholas were arrested and brought under guard to the district town. In the town they were committed to the prison.

II

A fortnight passed. Nicholas Yermolaiyevitch, the magistrate, was sitting in his office, turning over the papers of the Klausoff case; Dukovski was pacing restlessly up and down, like a wolf in a cage.

"You are convinced of the guilt of Nicholas and Psyekoff," he said, nervously plucking at his youthful beard. "Why will you not believe in the guilt of Maria Ivanovna?"

"I don't say I am not convinced. I am convinced, but somehow I don't believe it! There is no real proof, just theorizing."

"Very well, I'll prove it to you! You will stop sneering at the psychological side of the affair. To Siberia with your Maria Ivanovna! Just give me permission—"

"What are you going on about?"

"About the safety match! Have you forgotten it? I haven't!

I am going to find out who struck it in the murdered man's room. It was Maria Ivanovna. I will prove it to you. Just give me permission to go through the district to find out."

"That's enough! Sit down. Let us go on with the examination. Bring in Psyekoff!" ordered the examining magistrate.

They brought in Psyekoff. "Sit down, Psyekoff," said Chubikoff. "This is the last time I am going to talk to you. If you do not confess today, tomorrow will be too late. Come, tell me all—"

"I know nothing," answered Psyekoff, almost inaudibly.

"It's no use. Let me relate how the matter took place. On Saturday evening you were sitting in Klausoff's bedroom, drinking vodka and beer with him. Nicholas was waiting on you. At one o'clock, Marcus Ivanovitch announced his intention of going to bed. While he was taking off his boots, you and Nicholas seized your drunken master and threw him on the bed. One of you sat on his legs, the other on his head. Then a third person came in from the passage—a woman in a black dress, whom you know well, and who had previously arranged with you as to her share in your criminal deed. She seized a pillow and began to smother him.

"While the struggle was going on the candle went out. The woman took a box of safety matches from her pocket and lit the candle. After you had smothered him, and saw that he had ceased breathing, you and Nicholas pulled him out through the window and laid him down near the burdock. Fearing that he might come round again, you struck him with something sharp. Then you carried him away, and laid him down under a lilac bush for a short time. After resting awhile and considering what to do, you carried him across the fence. Well, what is the matter with you?"

34

"I am suffocating!" replied Psyekoff. "Very well—have it so. Only let me go out, please!"

"At last! He has confessed!" cried Chubikoff.

"And he doesn't deny the woman in the black dress!" exulted Dukovski. "But all the same, that safety match is tormenting me frightfully. Good-by! I am off!"

At six that evening Dukovski returned. It was clear that he did not come empty-handed.

"Listen, we have caught three already—isn't that so? Well, I have found the fourth," he declared, "and a woman at that. I went to Klausoff's village. I visited everywhere and asked for safety matches. Twenty times I lost faith, and twenty times I got it back again. Only an hour ago I got on the track. They gave me a packet of ten boxes. One box was missing. I asked, 'Who bought the other box?' She was the one! Well, come!"

"Come where?"

"To her, to murderer number four! Do you know who she is? Olga Petrovna, Marcus Ivanovitch's wife—his own wife— that's who it is! She is the person who bought the matchbox! She is head over heels in love with Klausoff, even after he refused to live in the same house with her, because she was always scolding his head off. He positively refused to stay in the same house. 'Hell hath no fury like a woman scorned.' But come along! Quick, or it will be dark. Come!"

The magistrate frowned, and undecidedly stretched his hand toward his cap. "Let us go!"

It was dark when the magistrate's carriage rolled up to the porch of the old country house in which Olga Petrovna had taken refuge with her brother. Chubikoff and Dukovski were met at the threshold by a tall buxom woman of twenty-three, with pitch-black eyebrows and full red lips. It was Olga

Petrovna herself, apparently not the least distressed by the recent tragedy.

"Oh, what a pleasant surprise!" she said, smiling broadly. "You have come from the examination?"

"Yes. We came here to ask you, respected madam, where Marcus Ivanovitch is, whom you murdered!"

"What? Marcus Ivanovitch murdered?" stammered Olga Petrovna. "I don't—understand!"

"I ask you in the name of the law! Where is Klausoff? We know all!"

"Who told you?" Olga Petrovna asked in a low voice, unable to endure Dukovski's glance. "Come," she said, wringing her hands. "I have him hidden in the bath house!"

Olga Petrovna took a key down from the wall and led her guests to the courtyard. In the darkness appeared the shadowy outlines of trees, and among the trees a little house with a crooked chimney.

Nearing the bath house, Chubikoff and Dukovski saw a huge padlock on the door. Olga Petrovna unfastened the padlock and let her guests into the bath house.

"Where is he—where is the murdered man?" asked the examining magistrate.

"On the top shelf," whispered Olga Petrovna, trembling.

Dukovski took the candle in his hand and climbed up to the top shelf of the sweating frame. There he saw a long human body lying motionless on a large feather bed. The body drew in a quick breath and stirred. It raised a hand, stretched itself, and lifted its head.

Dukovski raised his candle to the face of the unknown, and cried out. He recognized the gallant cavalryman Klausoff.

"You—Marcus Ivanovitch! Is it possible?"

"Yes, it is I. That's you, Dukovski? And who's that other mug down there? Great snakes! It's the examining magistrate! What fate has brought him here?" Klausoff rushed down and threw his arms around Chubikoff in a cordial embrace. "I am in captivity here, as you see. She carried me off and locked me up, and—well, I am living here in the deserted bath house like a hermit. I am fed. Next week I think I'll try to get out. I'm tired of it here!"

"Incomprehensible!" said Dukovski. "For Heaven's sake, how did your boot get in the garden?"

"And what do you want to know that for? It's none of your business! It is an interesting tale, brother, that of the boot! I didn't want to go with Olga. I don't like to be bossed. She came under the window and began to abuse me. I was a bit drunk, so I took a boot and heaved it at her. Teach her not to scold again! But it didn't! She climbed in at the window, lit the lamp, and began to thrash me. Then she dragged me over here and locked me in. She feeds me now—on love, vodka, and ham! But where are you off to, Chubikoff?"

The examining magistrate swore, and left the bath house. Dukovski followed him, crestfallen. When they reached home, Chubikoff threw his cap under the table, and shook himself. "You," said Chubikoff, turning to Dukovski and shaking his fist, "I won't forget this in a thousand years!"

"But the safety match? How could I know?"

"Choke yourself with your safety match!" Chubikoff shouted, "and don't let me see a trace of you!"

Dukovski sighed, took his hat, and went out.

THE STIR OUTSIDE THE CAFÉ ROYAL
A STORY OF MISS VAN SNOOP, DETECTIVE
by Clarence Rook

Although Clarence Rook wrote stories about the slums of urban London similar in style to Rudyard Kipling, he never achieved the fame and success that his contemporaries did. In fact, very little is known about Rook, except that he was born in 1863 and he first began his writing career as a journalist in 1896. He then wrote over the the next twelve years for journals such as The Daily Chronicle, The Globe, *and* The Chap-Book, *in the latter of which he interviewed one of his own admirers, the famous author George Bernard Shaw.*

Best known for his novel about the working class, The Hooligan Nights, *published in 1899, Rook died in London county on December 23, 1915, at the young age of fifty-two from "paralysis, bed sores, and exhaustion." His death certificate stated that his wife, Clare, was at his bedside, but there was no mention of any children.*

Although little is known about the man's life, one can see from his works that Rook had a fascination for human interaction of all kinds. In his short story "The Stir Outside the Café Royal," the author shows how his characters share his fascination through the animated actions of the young detective Miss Van Snoop. As you will see, this appropriately named sleuth is clearly driven by more than her love of justice when she captures her criminals.

Colonel Mathurin was one of the aristocrats of crime; at least Mathurin was the name under which he had accomplished a daring bank robbery in Detroit, which had involved the violent death of the manager. It was also generally believed by the police that the individual who was at the bottom of some long-firm frauds in Melbourne was none other than Mathurin under another name, and that the designer and chief gainer in a sensational murder case in the Midlands was the same mysterious and ubiquitous personage.

But Mathurin had for years eluded pursuit. Indeed, it was generally known that he was the most desperate among criminals, and was determined never to be taken alive. Moreover, as he invariably worked through subordinates who knew nothing of his whereabouts and were scarcely acquainted with his appearance, the police had but a slender clue to his identity.

As a matter of fact, only two people beyond his immediate associates in crime could have sworn to Mathurin if they had met him face to face. One of them was the Detroit bank manager, who he had shot with his own hand before the eyes of his fiancée. It was through the other that Mathurin was arrested, extradited to the States, and finally made to atone for his life of crime.

It all happened in a distressingly commonplace way, so far as the average spectator was concerned. But the story, which I have pieced together from the details supplied—firstly, by a certain detective sergeant whom I met in a tavern hard by Westminster, and secondly, by a certain young woman named Miss Van Snoop—has an element of romance, if you look below the surface.

It was about half-past one o'clock, on a bright and pleasant day, that a young lady was driving down Regent Street in a hansom which she had picked up outside her boardinghouse near Portland Road Station. She had told the cabman to drive slowly, as she was nervous behind a horse; and so she had leisure to scan, with the curiosity of a stranger, the strolling crowd that at nearly all hours of the day throngs Regent Street. It was a sunny morning, and everybody looked cheerful. Ladies were shopping, or looking in at the shop windows. Men about town were collecting an appetite for lunch; flower girls were selling "nice violets, sweet violets, penny a bunch"; and the girl in the cab leaned one arm on the apron and regarded the scene with alert attention. She was not exactly pretty, for the symmetry of her features was discounted by a hardness in the set of the mouth. But her hair, so dark as to be almost black, and her eyes of greyish blue set her beyond comparison with the commonplace.

Just outside the Café Royal there was a slight stir, and a temporary block in the foot traffic. A brougham was setting down, behind it was a victoria, and behind that a hansom; and as the girl glanced round the heads of the pair in the brougham, she saw several men standing on the steps. Leaning back suddenly, she opened the trapdoor in the roof.

"Stop here," she said, "I've changed my mind."

The driver drew up by the curb, and the girl skipped out.

"You shan't lose by the change," she said, handing him half-a-crown.

There was a tinge of American accent in the voice; and the cabman, pocketing the half-crown with thanks, smiled.

Meanwhile the girl walked slowly back toward the Café Royal, and with a quick glance at the men who were standing there, entered. One or two of the men raised their eyebrows; but the girl was quite unconscious, and went on her way.

"American, you bet," said one of the loungers. "They'll go anywhere and do anything."

Just in front of her as she entered was a tall, clean-shaven man, faultlessly dressed in glossy silk hat and frock-coat, with a flower in his buttonhole. He looked around for a moment in search of a convenient table. As he hesitated, the girl hesitated; but when the waiter waved him to a small table laid for two, the girl immediately sat down behind him at the next table.

"Excuse me, madam," said the waiter, "this table is set for four; would you mind—"

"I guess," said the girl, "I'll stay where I am." And the look in her eyes, as well as a certain sensation in the waiter's palm, ensured her against further disturbance.

The restaurant was full of people lunching, singly or in twos, in threes, and larger parties; and many curious glances were directed to the girl who sat at a table alone and pursued her way calmly through the menu. But the girl appeared to notice no one. When her eyes were off her plate they were fixed straight ahead—on the back of the man who had entered in front of her. The man, who had a half-bottle of champagne with his lunch, ordered a liqueur to accompany his coffee. The girl, who had drunk an aerated water, leaned back in her chair and wrinkled her brows. They were very straight brows, that seemed to meet over her nose when she wrinkled them in perplexity. Then she called a waiter.

"Bring me a sheet of notepaper," she said, "and my bill."

The waiter laid the sheet of paper before her, and the girl proceeded, after a few moments' thought, to write a few lines in pencil upon it. When this was done, she folded the sheet carefully and laid it in her purse. Then, having paid her bill, she returned her purse to her dress pocket, and waited patiently.

In a few minutes the clean-shaven man at the next table settled his bill and made preparation for departure. The girl at the same time pulled on her gloves, keeping her eyes upon her neighbor's back. As the man rose to depart and passed the table at which the girl had been sitting, the girl was looking into the mirror upon the wall and patting her hair. Then she turned and followed the man out of the restaurant, while a pair at an adjacent table remarked to one another that it was a curious coincidence for a man and woman to enter and leave at the same moment when they had no apparent connection.

But what happened outside was even more curious.

The man halted for a moment upon the steps at the entrance. The porter, who was in conversation with a policeman, turned, whistle in hand.

"Hansom, sir?" he asked.

"Yes," said the clean-shaven man.

The porter was raising his whistle to his lips when he noticed the girl behind.

"Do you wish for a cab, madam?" he asked, and blew upon his whistle.

As he turned again for an answer, he plainly saw the girl, who was standing close behind the clean-shaven man, slip her hand under his coat, and snatch from his hip pocket something which she quickly transferred to her own.

"Well, I'm—" began the clean-shaven man, swinging round and feeling in his pocket.

"Have you missed anything, sir?" said the porter, standing full in front of the girl to bar her exit.

"My cigarette case is gone," said the man, looking from one side to another.

"What's this?" said the policeman, stepping forward.

"I saw the woman's hand in the gentleman's pocket, plain as a pikestaff," said the porter.

"Oh, that's it, is it?" said the policeman, coming close to the girl. "I thought as much."

"Come now," said the clean-shaven man, "I don't want to make a fuss. Just hand back that cigarette case, and we'll say no more about it."

"I haven't got it," said the girl. "How dare you? I never touched your pocket."

The man's face darkened.

"Oh, come now!" said the porter.

"Look here, that won't do," said the policeman. "You'll have to come along with me. Better take a four-wheeler, eh, sir?"

For a knot of loafers, seeing something interesting in the wind, had collected round the entrance.

A four-wheeler was called, and the girl entered, closely followed by the policeman and the clean-shaven man.

"I was never so insulted in my life," said the girl.

Nevertheless, she sat back calmly in the cab, as though she was perfectly ready to face this or any other situation, while the policeman watched her closely to make sure that she did not dispose in any surreptitious way of the stolen article.

At the police station, the usual formalities were gone through, and the clean-shaven man was constituted prosecutor. But the girl stoutly denied being guilty of any offense.

The inspector in charge looked doubtful.

"Better search her," he said.

And the girl was led off to a room for an interview with the female searcher.

The moment the door closed the girl put her hand into her pocket, pulled out the cigarette case, and laid it upon the table.

"There you are," she said. "That will fix matters so far."

The woman looked rather surprised.

"Now," said the girl, holding out her arms, "feel in this other pocket, and find my purse."

The woman picked out the purse.

"Open it and read the note on the bit of paper inside."

On the sheet of paper which the waiter had given her, the girl had written these words, which the searcher read in a muttered undertone:

I am going to pick this man's pocket as the best way of getting him into a police station without violence. He is Colonel Mathurin, alias Rossiter, alias Connell, and he is wanted in Detroit, New York, Melbourne, Colombo, and London. Get four men to pin him unawares, for he is armed and desperate. I am a member of the New York detective force—Nora Van Snoop.

"It's all right," said Miss Van Snoop, quickly, as the searcher looked up at her after reading the note. "Show that to the boss—right away."

The searcher opened the door. After whispered consultation the inspector appeared, holding the note in his hand.

"Now then, be spry," said Miss Van Snoop. "Oh, you needn't worry! I've got my credentials right here," and she dived into another pocket.

"But do you know—can you be sure," said the inspector, "that this is the man who shot the Detroit bank manager?"

"Great heavens! Didn't I see him shoot Will Stevens with my own eyes! And didn't I take service with the police to hunt him out?"

The girl stamped her foot, and the inspector left. For two, three, four minutes, she stood listening intently. Then a shout reached her ears.

Two minutes later the inspector returned.

"I think you're right," he said. "We have found enough evidence on him to identify him. But why didn't you give him in charge before to the police?"

"I wanted to arrest him myself," said Miss Van Snoop, "and I have. Oh, Will! Will!"

Miss Van Snoop sank into a cane-bottomed chair, laid her head upon the table, and cried. She had earned the luxury of hysterics. In half an hour she left the station, and, proceeding to a post office, cabled her resignation to the detective force in New York.

THE RUBY AND THE CALDRON
by Anna Katharine Green

Born in 1846 in New York, Anna Katharine Green is known to many mystery readers as the mother, grandmother, and godmother of the detective story. Raised in Brooklyn by her mother, Katharine Ann Green, and her father, James Wilson Green, a well-known criminal lawyer, Green later attended Ripley Female College in Poultney, Vermont, where, after graduating, she met her future husband, Charles Rohlfs, a furniture designer and manufacturer. The couple had three children and spent most of their lives in Buffalo, New York, until her death in 1935.

Green's most famous work is The Leavenworth Case, *which was published in 1878. It was instantly successful and is still considered one of the best-selling detective novels ever written. In the novel, the author created her most brilliant sleuth, Ebenezer Gryce, who not only solves the case in this book but surfaces in many of Green's subsequent works, often accompanied by his equally capable female assistant, Amelia Butterworth.*

Written in the first person from the detective's point of view, "The Ruby and the Caldron" begins with the discovery of Mrs. Burton's missing valuable ruby by the greedy Mr. Deane. He and two young ladies are on their way to the Ashleys' grand ball, where Mr. Deane plans to turn in the gem for a reward. Imagine his despair, however, when Deane discovers that the ruby has been stolen once again . . .

from him! But was it really stolen? And just what was the small object that Miss Glover was seen picking up from the ground and putting into her dress?

———————————————

As there were two good men on duty that night, I did not see why I should remain at my desk, even though there was an unusual stir created in our small town by the grand ball given at The Evergreens.

But just as I was preparing to start for home, an imperative ring called me to the telephone and I heard:

"Halloo! Is this the police station?"

"It is."

"A detective is wanted at once at The Evergreens. He can not be too clever or too discreet. A valuable jewel has been lost, which must be found before the guests disperse for home. Large reward if the matter ends successfully and without too great publicity."

"May I ask who is speaking to me?"

"Mrs. Ashley."

It was the mistress of The Evergreens and giver of the ball.

"A man shall be sent at once. Where will you meet him?"

"In the butler's pantry at the rear. Let him give his name as Jennings."

"Very good. Good-by."

A pretty piece of work! Should I send Hendricks or should I send Hicks? Hendricks was clever and Hicks discreet, but neither united both qualifications in the measure demanded by the sensible and quietly-resolved woman with whom I had just been talking. What alternative remained? I must go myself.

It was not late—not for a ball night, at least—and as half the town had been invited to the dance, the streets were alive with carriages. I was watching the blink of their lights through the fast falling snow when my attention was drawn to a face which struck me as peculiar. These carriages were all coming my way instead of rolling in the direction of The Evergreens. Had they been empty this would have needed no explanation, but, as far as I could see, most of them were full, and that, too, with loudly talking women and gesticulating men. Something of a serious nature must have occurred at The Evergreens. Rapidly I paced on and soon found myself before the great gates.

Vehicles of all descriptions blocked the entrance. None seemed to be passing up the driveway; all stood clustered at the gates, and as I drew nearer I perceived many an anxious head thrust forth from their quickly opened doors and heard many an exclamation of disappointment as the short inter-change of words went on between the drivers of these various turnouts and a man drawn up in quiet resolution before the unexpectedly barred entrance.

Slipping round to this man's side, I listened to what he was saying. It was simple but very explicit.

"Mrs. Ashley asks everybody's pardon, but the ball can't go on tonight. Something has happened which makes the reception of further guests impossible. Tomorrow evening she will be happy to see you all. The dance is simply postponed."

This he had probably repeated forty times, and each time it had probably been received with the same mixture of doubt and curiosity which now held the lengthy procession in check.

Not wishing to attract attention, yet anxious to lose no time, I pressed up still nearer, and, bending toward him from the shadow cast by a convenient post, uttered: "Jennings."

Instantly he unlocked a small gate at his right. I passed in and proceeded to take my way to the house through the double row of evergreens bordering the semicircular approach.

As these trees stood very close together and were, besides, heavily laden with fresh-fallen snow, I failed to catch a glimpse of the building itself until I stood in front of it. Then I saw that it was brilliantly lighted, and gave evidence here and there of some festivity; but the guests were too few for the effect to be very exhilarating and, passing around to the rear, I sought the special entrance to which I had been directed.

A heavy-browed porch, before which stood a caterer's wagon, led me to a door which had every appearance of being the one I sought. Pushing it open, I entered, and speedily found myself in the midst of twenty or more waiters and chattering housemaids. To one of the former I addressed the question, "Where is the butler's pantry? I am told that I shall find the lady of the house there."

"Your name?" was the curt demand.

"Jennings."

"Follow me."

I was taken through narrow passages and across one or two store-rooms to a small but well-lighted closet, where I was left, with the assurance that Mrs. Ashley would presently join me. I had never seen this lady, but I had often heard her spoken of as a woman of superior character and admirable discretion.

She did not keep me waiting. The door opened and this fine, well-poised woman was telling her story in the straightforward manner I so much admire and so seldom meet with.

The article lost was a large ruby of singular beauty and great value—the property of Mrs. Burton, the senator's wife, in whose honor this ball was given. It had not been lost in the house nor had it been originally missed that evening. Mrs. Burton and herself had attended the great football game in the afternoon, and it was on the college campus that Mrs. Burton had first dropped her invaluable jewel.

But a reward of five hundred dollars having been at once offered to whomever should find and restore it, a great search had followed, which ended in its being picked up by one of the students and brought back as far as the great step leading up to the front door, when it had again disappeared, and in a way to rouse conjecture of the strangest and most puzzling character.

The young man who had brought it thus far bore the name of John Deane, and was a member of the senior class. He had been the first to detect its sparkle in the grass, and those who were near enough to see his face at that happy moment say that it expressed the utmost satisfaction at his good luck.

"You see," said Mrs. Ashley, "he has a sweetheart, and five hundred dollars looks like a fortune to a young man who is just starting life. But he was weak enough to take this girl into his confidence, and on their way here—for both were invited to the ball—he went so far as to pull it out of his pocket and show it to her.

"They were admiring it together and vaunting its beauties to the young lady friend who had accompanied them, when their carriage turned into the driveway and they saw the lights of the house flashing before them. Hastily restoring the jewel to the little bag he had made for it out of the finger-end of an old glove—a bag in which he assured me he had been careful to keep it safely tied ever since picking it up on the college green—he thrust it back into his pocket and prepared to help the ladies out.

But just then a disturbance arose in front. A horse which had been driven up was rearing in a way that threatened to overturn the light buggy to which he was attached. As the occupants of this buggy were ladies, and seemed to have no control over the beast, Deane naturally sprang to the rescue.

Bidding his own ladies alight and make for the porch, he hurriedly ran forward and, pausing in front of the maddened animal, waited for an opportunity to seize him by the rein. He says that as he stood there facing the beast with fixed eye and raised hand, he distinctly felt something strike or touch his breast. But the sensation conveyed no meaning to him in his excitement, and he did not think of it again till, the horse well in hand and the two alarmed occupants of the buggy rescued, he turned to see where his own ladies were, and beheld them looking down at him from the midst of a circle of young people, drawn from the house by the screaming of the women.

Instantly a thought of the treasure he carried recurred to his mind, and dropping the rein of the now quieted horse, he put his hand to his pocket. The jewel was gone. He declares that for a moment he felt as if he had been struck on the head by one of the hoofs of the frantic horse he had just handled. But immediately the importance of his loss and the necessity he felt for instant action restored him to himself, and shouting aloud, 'I have dropped Mrs. Burton's ruby!' begged everyone to stand still while he made a search for it.

"This all occurred, as you must know, more than an hour and a half ago, consequently before many of my guests had arrived. My son, who was one of the few spectators gathered on the porch, tells me that there was only one other carriage behind the one in which Mr. Deane had brought his ladies. Both of these had stopped short of the stepping-stone, and as

the horse and buggy which had made all this trouble had by this time been driven to the stable, nothing stood in the way of his search but the rapidly accumulating snow which, if you remember, was falling very thick and fast at the time.

"My son, who had rushed in for his coat, came running down with offers to help him. So did some others. But, with an imploring gesture, he begged to conduct the search alone, the ground being in such a state that the delicately-mounted jewel ran great risk of being trodden into the snow and thus injured or lost. They humored him for a moment, then, seeing that his efforts bade fair to be fruitless, my son insisted upon joining him, and the two looked the ground over, inch by inch, from the place where Mr. Deane had set foot to ground in alighting from his carriage to the exact spot where he had stood when he had finally seized hold of the horse. But no ruby.

"Then Harrison (that is my son's name) sent for a broom and went over the place again, sweeping aside the surface snow and examining the ground beneath, but with no better results than before. No ruby could be found. My son came to me panting. Mrs. Burton and myself stood awaiting him in a state of suspense. Guests and fete were alike forgotten. We had heard that the jewel had been found on the campus by one of the students and had been brought back as far as the step in front and then lost again in some unaccountable manner in the snow, and we hoped, nay expected from moment to moment, that it would be brought in.

"When Harrison entered, pale, disheveled, and shaking his head, Mrs. Burton caught me by the hand, and I thought she would faint. For this jewel is of far greater value to her than its mere worth in money, though that is by no means small.

"It is a family jewel and was given to her by her husband under special circumstances. He prizes it even more than she does, and he is not here to counsel her in this extremity. Besides, she was wearing it in direct opposition to his expressed wishes. This I must tell you, to show how imperative it is for us to recover it; also to account for the large reward she is willing to pay. When he last looked at it he noticed that the fastening was a trifle slack and, though he handed the trinket back, he told her distinctly that she was not to wear it till it had been either to Tiffany's or Starr's. But she considered it safe enough, and put it on to please the boys, and lost it. Senator Burton is a hard man, and in short, the jewel must be found. I give you just one hour in which to do it."

"But madam . . . " I protested.

"I know," she put in, with a quick nod and a glance over her shoulder to see if the door was shut. "I have not finished my story. Hearing what Harrison had to say, I took action at once. I bade him call in the guests, whom curiosity or interest still detained on the porch, and seat them in a certain room which I designated to him. Then, after telling him to send two men to the gates with orders to hold back all further carriages from entering, and two others to shovel up and cart away to the stable every particle of snow for ten feet each side of the front step, I asked to see Mr. Deane.

"But here my son whispered something into my ear, which it is my duty to repeat. It was to the effect that Mr. Deane believed that the jewel had been taken from him; he insisted, in fact, that he had felt a hand touch his breast while he awaited an opportunity to seize the horse.

"'Very good,' said I, 'we'll remember that, too; but first see that my orders are carried out and that all approaches to the grounds are guarded and no one allowed to come in or go out without permission from me.'

"He left us, and I was turning to encourage Mrs. Burton when my attention was caught by the eager face of a little friend of mine, who, quite unknown to me, was sitting in one of the corners of the room. She was studying my countenance in a sort of subdued anxiety, hardly natural in one so young, and I was about to call her to my side and question her when she made a sudden dive and vanished from the room. Some impulse made me follow her.

"She is a conscientious little thing, but timid as a hare, and though I saw she had something to say, it was with difficulty I could make her speak. Only after the solemn assurances that her name should not be mentioned in the matter would she give me the following information, which you may possibly think throws another light upon the affair.

"It seems that she was looking out of a front window when Mr. Deane's carriage drove up. She had been watching the antics of the horse attached to the buggy, but as soon as she saw Mr. Deane going to the assistance of those in danger, she let her eyes stray back to the ladies whom he had left behind him in the carriage.

"She did not know these ladies, but their looks and gestures interested her, and she watched them quite intently as they leaped to the ground and made their way toward the porch. One went on quickly and without pause to the step, but the other—the one who came last—did not. She stopped a moment, perhaps to watch the horse in front, perhaps to draw her cloak more closely about her, and when she again moved on, it was with a start and a hurried glance at her feet, terminating in a quick turn and a sudden stooping to the ground. When she again stood upright, she had something in her hand which she thrust furtively into her breast."

"How was this lady dressed?" I inquired.

"In a white cloak, with an edging of fur. I took pains to learn that, too, and it was with some curiosity, I assure you, that I examined the few guests who had now been admitted to the room I had so carefully pointed out to my son. Two of them wore white cloaks, but one of these was Mrs. Dalrymple, and I did not give her or her cloak a second thought. The other was a tall, fine-looking girl, with an air and bearing calculated to rouse admiration if she had not shown so very plainly that she was in a state of inner perturbation. Though she tried to look amiable and pleased, I saw that she had some care on her mind, which, had she been Mr. Deane's fiancée, would have needed no explanation; but as she was only Mr. Deane's fiancée's friend, its cause was not so apparent.

"The floor of the room, as I had happily remembered, was covered with crash, and as I lifted each garment off—I allowed no maid to assist me in this—I shook it well; ostensibly, because of the few flakes clinging to it, really to see if anything could be shaken out of it. Of course, I met with no success. I had not expected to, but it is my disposition to be thorough. These wraps I saw all hung in an adjoining closet, the door of which I locked—here is the key—after which I handed my guests over to my son who led them into the drawing room where they joined the few others who had previously arrived, and went myself to telephone to you."

I bowed and asked where the young people were now.

"Still in the drawing room. I have ordered the musicians to play, and consequently there is more or less dancing. But, of course, nothing can remove the wet blanket which has fallen over us all—nothing but the finding of this jewel. Do you see your way to accomplishing this? We are, from this moment, at your disposal; only I pray that you will make no more disturbance than is necessary, and, if possible, arouse no suspicions you cannot back up by facts. I dread a scandal almost as much as I do sickness and death, and these young people—well, their lives are all before them, and neither Mrs. Burton nor myself would wish to throw the shadow of a false suspicion over the least of them."

I assured her that I sympathized with her scruples and would do my best to recover the ruby without inflicting undue annoyance upon the innocent. Then I inquired whether it was known that a detective had been called in. She seemed to think it was suspected by some, if not by all. At which my way seemed a trifle complicated.

We were about to proceed when another thought struck me.

"Madam, you have not said if the carriage was searched."

"I forgot. Yes, the carriage was thoroughly overhauled, and before the coachmen left the box."

"Who did this overhauling?"

"My son. He would not trust any other hand than his own in a business of this kind."

"One more question, madam. Did anyone approach Mr. Deane on the carriage-drive prior to his assertion that the jewel was lost?"

"No. And there were no tracks in the snow of any such person. My son looked."

And I would look, or so I decided within myself, but I said nothing; and in silence we proceeded to the drawing room.

I had left my overcoat behind me, and always being well-dressed, I did not present so bad an appearance. Still I was not in party attire and could not pass for a guest if I had wanted to, which I did not. I felt that I must rely on insight in this case and on a certain power I had always possessed of reading faces. That the case called for just this species of intuition I was positive. Mrs. Burton's ruby was within a hundred yards of us at this very moment, probably within a hundred feet; but to lay hands on it and without scandal—well, that was a problem calculated to rouse the interest of even an old police officer like myself.

A strain of music, desultory, however, and spiritless, like everything else about the place that night, greeted us as Mrs. Ashley opened the door leading directly into the large front hall.

Immediately a scene meant to be festive, but which was, in fact, desolate, burst upon us. The lights, the flowers and the brilliant appearance of such ladies as flitted in from the parlors, were all suggestive of the cheer suitable to a great occasion. But in spite of this, the effect was altogether melancholy. For the hundreds who should have graced this scene, and for whom this illumination had been made and these festoons hung, had been turned away from the gates, and the few who felt they must remain, because their hostess showed no disposition to let them go, wore anything but holiday faces, despite their forced smiles and pitiful attempts at nonchalance and gaiety.

I scrutinized these faces carefully. I detected nothing in them but annoyance at a situation which certainly was anything but pleasant.

Turning to Mrs. Ashley, I requested her to be kind enough to point out her son, adding that I should be glad to have a moment's conversation with him, also with Mr. Deane.

"Mr. Deane is in one of those small rooms over there. He is quite upset. Not even Mrs. Burton can comfort him. My son—oh, there is Harrison!"

A tall, fine-looking young man was crossing the hall. Mrs. Ashley called him to her, and in another moment we were standing together in one of the empty parlors.

I gave him my name and told him my business. Then I said, "Your mother has allotted me an hour in which to find the valuable jewel which has just been lost on these premises." Here I smiled. "She evidently has confidence in my ability. I must see that I do not disappoint her."

All this time I was examining his face. It was handsome, as I have said, but it had also a very candid expression. The eyes looked straight into mine, and while showing some anxiety, betrayed no deeper emotion than the occasion called for.

"Have you any suggestions? I understand that you were on the ground almost as soon as Mr. Deane discovered his loss."

His eyes changed a trifle but did not swerve. Of course he had been informed by his mother of the suspicious action of the young lady who had been a member of that gentleman's party, and shrank, as anyone in his position would, from the responsibilities entailed by this knowledge.

"No," said he. "We have done all we can. The next move must come from you."

"There is one that will settle the matter," I assured him, still with my eyes scrutinizingly on his face. "It is a universal search, not of places, but of persons. But it is a harsh measure."

"A most disagreeable one," Harrison emphasized, his face flushing. "Such an indignity offered to guests would never be forgotten or forgiven."

"True, but if they offered to submit to this themselves?"

"They? How?"

"If you, the son of the house—their host we may say— should call them together and, for your own satisfaction, empty your pockets in the sight of everyone, don't you think that all the men, and possibly all the women too . . ." (here I let my voice fall suggestively) ". . . would be glad to follow suit? It could be done in apparent joke."

He shook his head with a straightforward air, which raised him high in my estimation.

"That would call for little but effrontery on my part," said he, "but think what it would demand from these boys who came here for the sole purpose of enjoying themselves. I will not so much as mention the ladies."

"Yet one of the latter . . . "

"I know," he quietly acknowledged, growing restless for the first time.

I withdrew my eyes from his face. I had learned what I wished. He did not shrink from search, therefore the jewel was not in his pockets. This left but two persons for suspicion. But I disclosed nothing of my thoughts. I merely asked pardon for a suggestion that, while pardonable in a man accustomed to handling crime with ungloved hands, could not fail to prove offensive to a gentleman like himself.

"We must move by means less open," I concluded. "It adds to our difficulties, but that cannot be helped. I should now like a glimpse of Mr. Deane."

"Do you not wish to speak to him?"

"I should prefer a sight of his face first."

He led me across the hall and pointed through an open door. In the center of a small room containing a table and some chairs, I perceived a young man sitting, with fallen head and dejected air, staring at vacancy. By his side, with hand laid on his, knelt a young girl, striving in this gentle but speechless way to comfort him. It made a pathetic picture. I drew Ashley away.

"I am disposed to believe in that young man," said I. "If he still has the jewel, he would not try to carry off the situation in just this way. He really looks broken-hearted."

"Oh, he is dreadfully cut up. If you could have seen how frantically he searched for the stone, and the depression into which he fell when he realized that it was not to be found, you would not doubt him for an instant. What made you think he might still have the ruby?"

"Oh, we police officers think of everything. Then the fact that he insists that something or someone touched his breast on the driveway strikes me as a trifle suspicious. Your mother says that no second person could have been there, or the snow would have given evidence of it."

"Yes, I looked expressly. Of course, the drive itself was full of hoof-marks and wheel-tracks, for several carriages had already passed over it. Then there were all of Deane's footsteps, but no other man's, as far as I could see."

"Yet he insists that he was touched or struck with no one there to touch or strike him."

Mr. Ashley was silent.

"Let us step out and take a view of the place," I suggested. "I should prefer doing this to questioning the young man in his present state of mind." Then, as we turned to put on our coats, I asked with suitable precaution: "Do you suppose that he has the same suspicions as ourselves, and that it is to hide these suspicions that he insists upon the jewel's having been taken away from him at a point the ladies approached?"

Young Ashley bent his somewhat startled eyes on mine.

"Nothing has been said to him of what Miss Peters saw Miss Glover do. I could not bring myself to mention it. I have not even allowed myself to believe . . . "

Here a fierce gust, blowing in from the door he had just opened, cut short his words, and neither of us spoke again till we stood on the exact spot in the driveway where the episode we were endeavoring to understand had taken place.

"Oh," I cried as soon as I could look about me, "the mystery is explained. Look at that bush, or perhaps you call it a shrub. If the wind were blowing as freshly as it is now, and very probably it was, one of those branches might easily be switched against his breast, especially if he stood, as you say he did, close against this border."

"Well, I'm a fool. Only the other day I told the gardener that these branches would need trimming in the spring, and yet I never so much as thought of them when Mr. Deane spoke of something striking his breast."

As we turned back I remarked: "With this explanation of the one doubtful point in his otherwise plausible account, we can credit his story as being in the main true, which," I calmly added, "places him above suspicion and narrows our inquiry down to one."

We had moved quickly and were now at the threshold of the door by which he had come out. "Mr. Ashley," I said, "I shall have to ask you to add to your former favors that of showing me the young lady in whom, from this moment on, we are especially interested. If you can let me see her first without her seeing me, I shall be infinitely obliged to you."

"I don't know where she is. I shall have to search for her."

"I will wait by the hall door."

In a few minutes he returned to me. "Come," said he, and led me into what I judged to be the library.

With a gesture toward one of the windows, he backed out, leaving me to face the situation alone. I was rather glad of this.

Glancing in the direction he had indicated, and perceiving the figure of a young lady standing with her back to me on the farther side of a flowing lace curtain, I took a few steps toward her, hoping that the movement would cause her to turn. But it entirely failed to produce this effect, nor did she give any sign that she noted the intrusion. This prevented me from catching the glimpse of her face which I so desired, and obliged me to confine myself to a study of her dress and attitude.

The former was very elegant, more elegant than the appearance of her two friends had led me to expect. Though I am far from being an authority on feminine dress, I did have experience enough to know that those sweeping folds of satin, with their festoons of lace and loops of shiny trimming, represented not only the best efforts of the dressmaker's art, but very considerable means on the part of the woman wearing such a gown. This was a discovery which altered the complexion of my thoughts for a moment; for I had presupposed her a girl of humble means, willing to sacrifice certain scruples to obtain a little extra money. This imposing figure might be that of a millionaire's daughter; how then could I associate her, even in my own mind, with theft? I decided that I must see her face before giving answer to these doubts.

She did not seem inclined to turn. She had raised the shade from before the wintry panes and was engaged in looking out. Her attitude was not that of one simply enjoying a moment's respite from the dance. It was rather that of an absorbed mind brooding upon what gave little or no pleasure. As I further gazed, I noted the droop of her lovely shoulders and the languor visible in her whole bearing, I began to regard a glimpse of her features as imperative. Moving forward, I came upon her suddenly.

"Excuse me, Miss Smith," I boldly exclaimed; then paused, for she had turned instinctively and I had seen that for which I had risked this daring move. "Your pardon," I apologized. "I mistook you for another young lady," and drew back a low bow to let her pass, for I saw that she thought only of escaping both me and the room.

And I did not wonder at this, for her eyes were streaming with tears, and her face, which was doubtless a pretty one under ordinary conditions, looked so distorted with emotions that she was no fit subject for any man's eye, let alone that of hard-hearted officer of the law on the lookout for the guilty hand which had just appropriated a jewel worth anywhere from eight to ten thousand dollars.

Yet I was glad to see her weep, for only first offenders weep, and first offenders are amenable to influence, especially if they have been led into wrong by impulse and are weak rather than wicked.

Anxious to make no blunder, I resolved, before proceeding further, to learn what I could of the character and antecedents of the suspected one, and this from the only source which offered—Mr. Deane's affianced.

This young lady was delicate, with a face like a flower. Recognizing her sensitive nature, I approached her with the utmost gentleness. Not seeking to disguise either the nature of my business or my reasons for being in the house, since all this gave me authority, I modulated my tone to suit her gentle spirit, and, above all, I showed the utmost sympathy for her lover, whose rights in the reward had been taken from him as certainly as the jewel had been taken from Mrs. Burton. In this way I gained her confidence, and she was quite ready to listen when I observed, "There is a young lady here who seems to be in a state of even greater trouble than Mr. Deane. Why is this? You brought her here. Is her sympathy with Mr. Deane so great as to cause her to weep over his loss?"

"Frances? Oh, no. She likes Mr. Deane and she likes me, but not well enough to cry over our misfortunes. I think she has some trouble of her own."

"One that you can tell me?"

Her surprise was manifest.

"Why do you ask that? What interest have you (called in, as I understand, to recover a stolen jewel) in Frances Glover's personal difficulties?"

I saw that I must make my position perfectly plain.

"Only this. She was seen to pick up something from the driveway, where no one else had succeeded in finding anything."

"She? When? Who saw her?"

"I cannot answer all these questions at once. She was seen to do this—no matter by whom—during your passage from the carriage to the stoop. As you preceded her, you naturally did not observe this action, which was fortunate, perhaps, as you would scarcely have known what to do or say about it."

"Yes, I should," she retorted, with a most unexpected display of spirit. "I should have insisted upon an answer. I love my friends, but I love the man I am to marry, better." Here her voice fell and a most becoming blush suffused her cheek.

"Quite right," I assented. "Now will you answer my former question? What troubles Miss Glover? Can you tell me?"

"That I cannot. I only know that she has been very silent since she left the house. I thought her beautiful new dress would please her, but it does not seem to. She has been unhappy and preoccupied all the evening. She only roused a bit when Mr. Deane showed us the ruby and said—Oh, I forgot!"

"What's that? What have you forgot?"

"What you said just now. I wouldn't add a word—"

"Pardon me!" I interrupted, looking as fatherly as I could. "But you have added this word and now you must tell me what it means. You were going to say she showed interest in—"

"In what Mr. Deane said about the reward. That is, she looked eagerly at the ruby and sighed when he acknowledged that he expected it to bring him five hundred dollars before midnight. But any girl of no more means than she might do that. It would not be fair to lay too much stress on a sigh."

"Is not Miss Glover wealthy? She wears a very expensive dress, I observe."

"I know it and I have wondered a little at it, for her father is not very well off. But perhaps she bought it with her own money; I know she has some; she is an artist in burnt wood."

I left the subject of Miss Glover's dress shop. I had heard enough to satisfy me that my first theory was correct. This young woman, beautifully dressed, and with a face from which the rounded lines of early girlhood had not yet departed, held in her possession, probably at this very moment, Mrs. Burton's magnificent jewel. But where? On her person or hidden in her belongings? I remembered the cloak in the closet and thought it wise to assure myself that the jewel was not secreted in this garment, before I proceeded to extreme measures. Mrs. Ashley, upon being consulted, agreed with me, and presently, I had this poor girl's cloak in my hands.

Did I find the ruby? No, but I found something else tucked away in an inner pocket which struck me as bearing quite pointedly upon this case.

It was the bill—crumpled, soiled and tear-stained—of the dress whose elegance had surprised her friends and made me, for a short time, regard her as the daughter of wealthy parents. An enormous bill, which must have struck dismay in the soul of this self-supporting girl, who probably had no idea of how a French dressmaker charges for items. Four hundred and fifty dollars! And for one gown! I declare I felt indignant myself and could understand why she heaved that sigh when Mr. Deane spoke of the five hundred dollars he expected from Mrs. Burton, and later, how she succumbed to the temptation of making the effort to secure this sum for herself when, in following the latter's footsteps up the driveway, she stumbled upon this same jewel fallen, as it were, from his pocket into her very hands. The impulse of the moment was so strong and the consequences so little anticipated!

It is not at all probable that she foresaw he would shout aloud his loss and draw the whole household out on the porch. Of course when he did this, the feasibility of her project was gone, and I only wished that I had been present and able to note her countenance, as, crowded in with others on that windy porch, she watched the progress of the search. Every moment of it must have caused her to feel, if she had been as well brought up as all indication showed, that it was a dishonest act of which she had been guilty and that, willing or not, she must look upon herself as a thief so long as she held the jewel back from Mr. Deane or its rightful owner. But how face the publicity of restoring it now, after this elaborate and painful search, in which even the son of her hostess had taken part?

That would be to proclaim her guilt and thus effectually ruin her in the eyes of everybody concerned. No, she would keep the compromising article a little longer, in the hope of finding some opportunity of returning it without risk to her good name. And so she allowed the search to proceed.

I have entered thus elaborately into the supposed condition of this girl's mind on this critical evening, that you may understand why I felt a certain sympathy for her, which forbade harsh measures. I was sure, from the glimpse I had caught of her face, that she longed to be relieved from the tension she was under, and that she would gladly rid herself of this valuable jewel if she only knew how. This opportunity I proposed to give her; and this is why, on returning the bill to its place, I assumed such an air of relief on rejoining Mrs. Ashley.

She saw, and drew me aside.

"You have not found it!" she said.

"No," I returned, "but I am positive where it is."

"And where is that?"

"Over Miss Glover's uneasy heart."

Mrs. Ashley turned pale.

"Wait," said I. "I have a scheme for getting it without making her shame public. Listen!" Then I whispered a few words in her ear.

She surveyed me in amazement for a moment, nodded, and then her face lit up.

"You are certainly earning your reward," she declared; and summoning her son, who was never far away from her side, she whispered her wishes. He started, bowed and hurried from the room.

By this time my business in the house was well-known to all, and I could not appear in hall or parlor without a great silence falling upon everyone present, followed by a breaking up of the only too small circle of unhappy guests into agitated groups. But I appeared to see nothing of all this till the proper moment, when, turning suddenly upon them all, I cried out cheerfully, but with a certain deference I thought would please them:

"Ladies and gentlemen, I have an interesting fact to announce. The snow which was taken up from the driveway has been put to melt in the great feed caldron over the stable fire. We expect to find the ruby at the bottom, and Mrs. Ashley invites you to be present at its recovery. She thought you might enjoy the excitement of watching the water ladled out."

A dozen girls bounded forward.

"Oh, yes, what fun! Where are our cloaks and our rubbers?"

Two only stood hesitating. One of these was Mr. Deane's lady love and the other her friend, Miss Glover. The former, perhaps, secretly wondered. The latter—but I dared not look long enough or closely enough in her direction to judge just what her emotions were. Presently these, too, stepped forward into the excited circle of young people, and were met by the two maids who were bringing in their wraps. Amid the bustle which now ensued, I caught sight of Mr. Deane's face peering from an open doorway. It was all alive with hope. I also perceived a lady looking down from the second story, who, I felt sure, was Mrs. Burton herself. Evidently my confident tone had produced more effect than the words themselves. Everyone looked upon the jewel as already recovered and regarded my invitation to the stable as a ruse by which I hoped to restore universal good feeling by giving them all a share in my triumph.

All but one! Nothing could make Miss Glover look otherwise than anxious, restless, and unsettled, and though she followed in the wake of the rest, it was with hidden face and lagging step, as if she recognized the whole thing as a farce and doubted her own power to go through it calmly.

"Ah, ha!" thought I. "Only be patient, my lady, and you will see what I shall do for you." And indeed I thought her eye brightened as we all drew up around the huge caldron standing full of water over the stable stove. As pains had already been taken to put out the fire in this stove, the ladies were not afraid of injuring their dresses and consequently crowded as close as their numbers would permit.

Miss Glover especially stood within reach of the brim, and as soon as I noted this, I gave the signal which had been agreed upon between Mr. Ashley and myself. Instantly the electric lights went out, leaving the place in total darkness.

A scream from the girls, laughter from their escorts, mingled with apologies from their seemingly mischievous host, filled up the interval of darkness which I had insisted should not be too soon curtailed. Then the lights glowed as suddenly as they had gone out, and while the glare was fresh on every face, I stole a glance at Miss Glover to see if she had made good use of the opportunity just accorded her for ridding herself of the jewel by dropping it into the caldron. If she had, both her troubles and mine were at an end; if she had not, then I need feel no further scruple in approaching her with the question I had hitherto found so difficult to put.

She stood with both hands grasping her cloak which she had drawn tightly about the rich folds of her expensive dress, but her eyes were fixed straight before her with a soft light in their depths which made her positively beautiful.

The jewel is in the pot, I inwardly decided, and ordered the two waiting stablemen to step forward with their ladles. Quickly those ladles went in, but before they could be lifted out dripping, half the ladies had scurried back, afraid of injury to their pretty dresses. But they soon sidled forward again, and watched with beaming eyes the slow but sure emptying of the great caldron at whose bottom they anticipated finding the lost jewel.

As the ladles were plunged deeper and deeper, the heads drew closer and so great was the interest shown, that even the busiest lips forgot to chatter, and eyes, whose only business up till now had been to follow with shy curiosity every motion made by their handsome young host, now settled on the murky depths of the great pot whose bottom was almost in sight.

As I heard the ladles strike this bottom, I instinctively withdrew a step in anticipation of the loud hurrah which would naturally hail the first sight of the lost ruby. Conceive then my chagrin, my bitter and mortified disappointment, when, after one look at the broad surface of the now exposed bottom, the one shout which rose was: "Nothing!"

I was so thoroughly put out that I did not wait to hear the complaints that burst from every lip. Drawing Mr. Ashley aside (who, by the way, seemed as much affected as myself by the turn affairs had taken) I remarked to him that there was only one course left open to us.

"And what is that?"

"To ask Miss Glover to show me what she picked up from your driveway."

"And if she refuses?"

"To take her quietly with me to the station, where we have women who can make sure that the ruby is not on her person."

Mr. Ashley made an involuntary gesture of repugnance.

"Let us pray that it will not come to that," he objected hoarsely. "Such a fine figure of a girl! Did you notice how bright and happy she looked when the lights sprang up? I declare she struck me as lovely."

"So she did me, and caused me to draw some erroneous conclusions. I shall have to ask you to procure me an interview with her as soon as we return to the house."

"She shall meet you in the library."

But when, a few minutes later, she joined me in the room just designated and I had full opportunity for reading her countenance, I own that my task became suddenly hateful to me. She was not far from my own daughter's age and, had it not been for her furtive look of care, appeared almost as blooming and bright. Would it ever come to pass that a harsh man of the law would feel it his duty to speak to my Flora as I must now speak to the young girl before me? The thought made me inwardly recoil and it was in as gentle a manner as possible that I made my bow and began with the following:

"I hope you will pardon me, Miss Glover. I hate to disturb your pleasure—" (this with the tears of alarm and grief rising in her eyes) "but you can tell me something which will greatly simplify my task and possibly put matters in such shape that you and your friends can be released to your homes."

"I?" She stood before me with amazed eyes, the color rising in her cheeks. I had to force my next words which, out of consideration for her, I made as direct as possible.

"Yes, miss. What was the article you were seen to pick up from the driveway soon after leaving your carriage?"

She started, then stumbled backward, tripping in her long train. "I pick up?" she murmured. Then with a blush, whether of anger or pride I could not tell, she coldly answered, "Oh, that was something of my own—something I had just dropped. I had rather not tell you what it was."

I scrutinized her closely. She met my eyes squarely, yet not with just the clear light I should, remembering Flora, have been glad to see there.

"I think it would be better for you to be entirely frank," said I. "It was the only article known to have been picked up from the driveway after Mr. Deane's loss of the ruby; and though we do not presume to say that it was the ruby, yet the matter would look clearer to us all if you would frankly state what this object was."

Her whole body seemed to collapse and she looked as if about to sink.

"Where is Minnie? Where is Mr. Deane?" she moaned, turning and staring at the door, as if she hoped they would fly to her aid. Then, in a burst of indignation, which I was fain to believe real, she turned on me with the cry, "It was a bit of paper which I had thrust into the bosom of my gown. It fell—"

"Your dressmaker's bill?" I intimated.

She stared, laughed hysterically for a moment, then sank upon a nearby sofa, sobbing spasmodically.

"Yes," she cried, after a moment, "my dressmaker's bill. You seem to know all my affairs."

Then suddenly, and with a startling impetuosity, which drew her to her feet, she added, "Are you going to tell everybody that? Are you going to state publicly that Miss Glover brought an unpaid bill to the party and that because Mr. Deane was unfortunate enough or careless enough to drop and lose the jewel he was bringing to Mrs. Burton, she is to be looked upon as a thief, because she stooped to pick up this bill which had slipped inadvertently from its hiding place? I shall die if you do," she cried. "I shall die if it is already known," she pursued, with increasing emotion. "Is it? Is it?"

Her passion was so great, so much greater than any likely to rise in a breast wholly innocent, that I began to feel very sober.

"No one but Mrs. Ashley and possibly her son know about the bill," said I, "and no one shall, if you will go with that lady to her room, and make plain to her, in the only way you can, that the extremely valuable article which has been lost tonight is not in your possession."

She threw up her arms with a scream. "I cannot! I cannot! Oh, I shall die of shame!" And she burst from the room like one distraught.

But in another moment she came cringing back. "I cannot face them," she said. "They all believe it; they will always believe it unless I submit—Oh, why did I ever come to this dreadful place? Why did I order this hateful dress which I can never pay for and which, in spite of the misery it has caused me, has failed to bring me the—"

She did not continue. She had caught my eye and seen there, perhaps, some evidence of the pity I could not but experience for her. With a sudden change of tone she advanced upon me with the appeal, "Save me from this humiliation. I have not seen the ruby. I am as ignorant of its whereabouts as—as Mr. Ashley himself. Won't you believe me? Won't they be satisfied if I swear—"

I was sorry for her. I began to think that some dreadful mistake had been made. Her manner seemed too ingenuous for guilt. Yet where could that ruby be, if not with this young girl? All other possibilities had been exhausted, and her story of the bill, even if accepted, would never quite exonerate her from secret suspicion while that elusive jewel remained unfound.

"You give me no hope," she moaned. "I must go out before them all and ask to have it proved that I am no thief. Oh, if God would have pity—"

"Or someone would find—Halloo! What's that?"

A shout had risen from the hall beyond.

She gasped and we both plunged forward. Mr. Ashley, still in his overcoat, stood at the other end of the hall, and facing him were the young people I had left scattered about in the various parlors. I thought he looked peculiar; his appearance differed from that of a quarter of an hour before, and when he glanced our way and saw who was standing with me in the library doorway, his voice took on a tone which made me doubt whether he was about to announce good news or bad.

But his first word settled that question.

"Rejoice with me!" he cried. "The ruby has been found! Do you want to see the culprit? Shall we bring him in?"

"Yes, yes," cried several voices, among them that of Mr. Deane, who now strode forward with beaming eyes. But some of the ladies looked frightened, and Mr. Ashley, noting this, glanced for encouragement toward us.

He seemed to find it in Miss Glover's eyes. She'd quivered and nearly fallen, but had drawn herself up by this time and was awaiting his further action in a fever of relief and hope which perhaps no one but myself could fully appreciate.

"A vile thief! A most unconscionable rascal!" vociferated Mr. Ashley. "You must see him, mother; you must see him, ladies, else you will not realize our good fortune. Open the door there and bring in the robber!"

At this command, uttered in ringing tones, the huge leaves of the great front door swung slowly forward, revealing the sturdy forms of the two stablemen holding down by main force the towering figure of—a horse!

The scream of astonishment which went up from all sides, united to Mr. Ashley's shout of hilarity, caused the animal, unused, no doubt, to drawing-rooms, to rear the length of his bridle. At which Mr. Ashley laughed again and gaily cried, "Confound the fellow! Look at him, mother; look at him ladies! Do you not see guilt written on his brow? It is he who has made us all this trouble. First, he must needs take umbrage at the two lights with which we presumed to illuminate our porch; then, envying Mrs. Burton her ruby and Mr. Deane his reward, seek to rob them both by grinding his hoofs all over the snow of the driveway till he came upon the jewel which Mr. Deane had dropped from his pocket, and taking it up in a ball of snow, secrete it in his left hind shoe—where it might be yet, if Mr. Spencer—" He bowed to a strange gentleman who at that moment entered. "Had not come himself for his daughters, and going first to the stable, found his horse so restless and seemingly lame—(There, boys, you may take the wretch now and harness him, but first hold up that guilty left hind hoof for the ladies to see.)—that he stooped to examine him, and so came upon this."

Here the young gentleman brought forward his hand. In it was a nondescript little wad, well soaked and shapeless; but once he had untied it, such a ray of rosy light burst from his outstretched palm that I doubt if a single woman there noted the clatter of the retiring beast or the heavy clang made by the two front doors as they shut upon the robber. Eyes and tongues were too busy, and Mr. Ashley, realizing that the interest of all present would remain, for a few minutes at least, with this marvelous jewel so astonishingly recovered, laid it, with many expressions of thankfulness, in Mrs. Burton's now eagerly outstretched palm, and advancing toward us, paused in front of Miss Glover and eagerly held out his hand.

The poor young thing, in trying to smile, had turned as white as a sheet. Before either of us could interpose an arm, she had slipped to the floor in a dead faint. With a murmur of pity and possibly of inward contrition, he stooped over her and together we carried her into the library, where I left her in his care, confident, from certain indications, that my presence would not be greatly missed by either of them.

Whatever hope I may have had of reaping the reward offered by Mrs. Ashley was now lost, but, in the satisfaction I experienced at finding this young girl as innocent as my Flora, I did not greatly care.

Well, it all ended more happily than may here appear. The horse not putting in his claim to the reward, and Mr. Spencer repudiating all right to it, it was paid in full to Mr. Deane, who went home in as buoyant a state of mind as was possible to him after the great anxieties of the preceding two hours. Miss Glover was sent back by the Ashleys in their own carriage, and I was told that Mr. Ashley declined to close the carriage door upon her till she had promised to come again the following night.

Anxious to make amends as I could for my share in the mortification she'd been subjected, I visited her in the morning, with a suggestion or two in regard to that little bill. But she met my first advance with a radiant smile and the exclamation, "Oh, I have settled all that! I have just come from Madame Dupré's. I told her that I had never imagined the dress could cost more than a hundred dollars, and I offered her that sum if she would take the dress back. And she did!"

I made a note of this dressmaker's name. She and I may have a bone to pick some day. But I said nothing to Miss Glover. I merely exclaimed, "And tonight?"

"Oh, I have an old spotted muslin. With a few flowers, it will make me look festive enough. One does not need fine clothes when one is—happy."

The dreamy far-off smile with which she finished the sentence was more eloquent than words, and I was not surprised when some time later I read of her engagement to Mr. Ashley.

But it was not till she could sign herself with his name that she told me just what underlay the misery of that night. She had met Harrison Ashley more than once before, and, though she did not say so, had evidently conceived an admiration for him which made her especially desirous of attracting and pleasing him.

Not understanding the world very well, certainly having very little knowledge of the tastes and feelings of wealthy people, she conceived that the more brilliantly she was attired the more likely she would be to please this rich young man. So in a moment of weakness she decided to devote all her small savings (a hundred dollars, as we know) to buying a gown so she could appear at his house without shame.

It came home, as dresses from French dressmakers are very apt to do, just in time for her to put it on for the party. The bill came with it, and when she saw the amount, she was so overwhelmed that she nearly fainted. But she could not give up her ball; so she dressed herself, and, being urged all the time to hurry, hardly stopped to give one look at the new and splendid dress which had cost so much.

The bill—the incredible, the enormous bill—was all she could think of, and the figures, which represented nearly her whole year's earnings, danced constantly before her eyes. She was ruined; but the ball, and Mr. Ashley—these still awaited her; so presently she worked herself up to some anticipation of enjoyment, and, having thrown on her cloak, was turning down her light preparatory to departure, when her eye fell on the bill lying open on her dresser.

It would never do to leave it there—never do to leave it anywhere in her room. There were prying eyes in the house, and she was as ashamed of that bill as she might have been of a contemplated theft. So she tucked it in her corsage and went down to join her friends in the carriage.

The rest we know, all but one small detail which turned to gall whatever enjoyment she was able to get out of the early evening. There was a young girl present, dressed in a simple muslin gown. While looking at it and inwardly contrasting it with her own splendor, Mr. Ashley passed by with another gentleman and she heard him say, "How much better young girls look in simple white than in the elaborate silks suitable for their mothers!"

Thoughtless words, possibly forgotten as soon as uttered, but they sharply pierced this already sufficiently stricken and uneasy breast and were the cause of the tears which had aroused my suspicion when I came upon her in the library.

But who can say, if the evening had been devoid of these occurrences and no emotions of contrition and pity had been awakened in her behalf in the breast of her chivalrous host, whether she would ever have become Mrs. Ashley?

A CURIOUS EXPERIENCE
by Mark Twain

*Mark Twain, whose real name was Samuel Clemens, was as well
known for his flamboyant personality as for his incredible wit. Born in
Florida, Missouri, on November 30, 1835, and moving to Hannibal
in that same state when he was four, Twain was fascinated by life on
the river, and many of his most famous works take place with a river as
the backdrop. In fact, he was even trained as a steamboat pilot, and it
was from this experience that the author created the name Mark Twain,
which means two fathoms in riverboat terms.*

*After working as a journalist for The Hannibal Journal, Twain
moved out west during the Civil War and spent many years in Nevada
and California, where he began his career as an author. After the war,
Charles Henry Webb published Twain's first book,* The Celebrated
Jumping Frog of Calaveras County, *in 1867. A few years later, now
a somewhat established writer, Twain married Olivia L. Langdon on
February 2, 1870.*

*Frequently lecturing across the country, Twain's face soon became as
familiar as his works, the most famous of which were* The Adventures
of Tom Sawyer, *published in 1876, and* The Adventures of
Huckleberry Finn, *published in 1884.*

*But while his career remained successful, Twain's personal life was
often difficult. He had several periods of financial difficulty, and in
1896 his oldest daughter, Susy, died, followed by his wife in 1904 and
his youngest daughter, Jean, in 1909. After their deaths, the infamous*

author could no longer bear to live in the same house in Hartford, Connecticut, where his family had spent so many happy years, so Twain built a house in Redding, Connecticut, where he spent some of his most productive writing years.

Visiting friends, attending plays, delivering speeches, granting interviews, and of course writing, Twain, one of the most well-known public figures of his time, was active until his death, April 21, 1910.

Twain was notable for displaying his love of deception and surprise endings in most of his work, and "A Curious Experience" is no exception. Here Twain tells the tale of a boy who has sent an entire Union regiment into a state of panic when it is thought that he is a dangerous spy for the confederacy. But is he? Read on and discover the truth.

In the winter of 1862-63 I was commandant of Fort Trumball, at New London, Conn. Maybe our life there was not so brisk as life at "the front"; still it was brisk enough, in its way—one's brains didn't cake together there for lack of something to keep them stirring. For one thing, all the Northern atmosphere at that time was thick with mysterious rumors—rumors to the effect that rebel spies were flitting everywhere, and getting ready to blow up our Northern forts, burn our hotels, send infected clothing into our towns, and all that sort of thing. All this had a tendency to keep us awake, and knock the traditional dullness out of garrison life. Besides, ours was a recruiting station—which is the same as saying we hadn't any time to waste in dozing, or dreaming, or fooling around. Why, with all our watchfulness, fifty percent of a day's recruits would leak out of our hands and give us the slip the same night. The bounties were so prodigious that a recruit could pay a sentinel three or four hundred dollars to let him escape, and still have enough of his bounty left to constitute a fortune for a poor man. Yes, our life was not drowsy.

Well, one day I was in my quarters, doing some writing, when a pale and ragged lad of fourteen or fifteen entered, made a neat bow, and said, "I believe recruits are received here? Will you please enlist me, sir?"

"Dear me, no! You are too young, my boy, and too small."

A disappointed look came into his face. He turned slowly away, as if to go; hesitated, then faced me again, and said, in a tone that went to my heart, "I have no home, and not a friend in the world. If you could only enlist me!"

But of course the thing was out of the question, and I said so as gently as I could. Then I told him to sit down by the stove and warm himself, and added, "You shall have something to eat, presently. You are hungry?"

He did not answer; he did not need to; the gratitude in his big, soft eyes was more eloquent than any words. He sat down by the stove, and I went on writing. I became absorbed in my work by and by, and forgot all about the boy. I don't know how long this lasted, but at length I happened to look up. "God bless my soul!" I said to myself. "I forgot the poor rat was starving." Then I made amends for my brutality by saying to him, "Come along, my lad; you shall dine with me; I am alone today."

He gave me another one of those grateful looks, and a happy light broke in his face. At the table he stood with his hand on his chair-back until I was seated, then seated himself.

As our meal progressed I observed that young Wicklow— Robert Wicklow was his full name—was of good breeding; never mind the details. We talked mainly about himself, and I had no difficulty in getting his history out of him. Briefly, this was little Wicklow's history:

When the war broke out, he and his invalid aunt and his father were living near Baton Rouge, on a great plantation which had been in the family for fifty years. The father was a Union man. He was persecuted in all sorts of ways, but clung to his principles. At last one night masked men burned his mansion down, and the family had to fly for their lives. They were hunted from place to place, and learned all there was to know about poverty, hunger, and distress. The invalid aunt found relief at last: misery and exposure killed her and she died in an open field, the rain beating upon her and the thunder booming overhead. Not long afterward the father was captured by an armed band; and while the son begged and pleaded, the victim was strung up before his face. As soon as the father was pronounced dead, the son was told that if he was not out of that region within twenty-four hours it would go hard with him.

That night he crept to the riverside and hid himself near a plantation landing. By and by the Duncan F. Kenner stopped there, and he swam out and concealed himself in the yawl that was dragging at her stern. Before daylight the boat reached the Stock Landing and he slipped ashore. He walked the three miles which lay between that point and the house of an uncle of his in Good-Children Street, in New Orleans, and then his troubles were over for the time being. But this uncle was a Union man, too, and before long he concluded that he had better leave the South. So he and young Wicklow slipped out of the country on board a sailing-vessel, and in due time reached New York. They put up at the Astor House. Young Wicklow had a good time of it for a while, strolling up and down Broadway, and observing the strange Northern sights; but in the end a change came—and not for the better. The uncle had been cheerful at first, but now he began to look troubled and despondent; moreover, he became moody and irritable; talked of money giving out, and no way to get more—"not enough left for one, let alone two." Then, one morning, he was missing—didn't come to breakfast. The boy inquired at the office, and was told that the uncle had paid his bill the night before and gone away—to Boston, the clerk believed, but was not certain.

The lad was alone and friendless. He did not know what to do, but concluded he had better try to follow and find his uncle. He went down to the steamboat landing: learned that the trifle of money in his pocket would not carry him to Boston; however, it would carry him to New London; so he took passage for that port, resolving to trust to Providence to furnish him means to travel the rest of the way. He had now been wandering about the streets of New London three days and nights, getting a bite and a nap here and there for charity's sake. But he had given up at last; courage and hope were both gone. If he could enlist, nobody could be more thankful; if he could not get in as a soldier, couldn't he be a drummer-boy? Ah, he would work so hard to please, and would be so grateful!

Well, there's the history of young Wicklow, just as he told it to me, barring details. I said, "My boy, you are among friends now—don't you be troubled any more."

How his eyes glistened! I called in Sergeant John Rayburn from Hartford, and said, "Rayburn, quarter this boy with the musicians. I am going to enroll him as a drummer-boy, and I want you to look after him and see that he is well treated."

Well, of course, interaction between the commandant of the post and the drummer-boy came to an end now; but the poor little friendless chap lay heavy on my heart just the same. I kept on the lookout, hoping to see him brighten up and begin to be cheery and gay; but no, the days went by, and there was no change. He associated with nobody; he was always absent-minded, always thinking; his face was always sad.

But now comes Sergeant Rayburn, one day, and says, "That new boy acts mighty strange, sir. He's all the time writin'."

"Writing? What does he write—letters?"

"I don't know, sir; but whenever he's off duty, he's nosin' around the fort, all by himself—blest if I think there's a hole or corner in it he hasn't been into—and every little while he outs with pencil and paper and scribbles somethin' down."

This gave me a most unpleasant sensation. I wanted to scoff at it, but it was not a time to scoff at anything that had the least suspicious tinge. Things were happening all around us in the North then that warned us to be always on the alert, and always suspecting. I recalled to mind the suggestive fact that this boy was from the South—the extreme South, Louisiana—and the thought was not of a reassuring nature, under the circumstances. Nevertheless, it cost me a pang to give the orders which I now gave to Rayburn. I felt like a father who plots to expose his own child to shame and injury. I told Rayburn to keep quiet, bide his time, and get me some of those writings whenever he could manage it without the boy's finding out. And I charged him not to do anything which might let the boy discover that he was being watched. I also ordered that he allow the lad his usual liberties, but that he be followed at a distance when he went out into the town.

During the next two days Rayburn reported to me several times. No success. The boy was still writing, but he always pocketed his paper with a careless air whenever Rayburn appeared in the vicinity. He had gone twice to an old deserted stable in the town, remained a minute or two, and come out again. One could not pooh-pooh these things—they had an evil look. I was obliged to confess to myself that I was getting uneasy. I went into my quarters and sent for my second in command—an officer of intelligence and judgment, son of General James Watson Webb. He was surprised and troubled. We had a long talk over the matter, and came to the conclusion that it would be worthwhile to institute a secret search. I determined to take charge of that myself. So I had myself called at two in the morning; and soon I was in the musicians' quarters, crawling along the floor among the snorers. I reached my slumbering waif's bunk at last, without disturbing anybody, captured his clothes and kit, and crawled stealthily back again.

When I got to my quarters, I found Webb there, eager to know the result. We made search immediately. The clothes were a disappointment. In the pockets we found blank paper and a pencil; nothing else, except a jackknife and such queer odds and ends and useless trifles as boys hoard and value. We turned to the kit hopefully. Nothing else there but a rebuke for us!—a little Bible with this written on the fly-leaf: "Stranger, be kind to my boy, for his mother's sake."

I looked at Webb—he dropped his eyes; he looked at me—I dropped mine. Neither spoke. I put the book reverently back in its place. Presently Webb went away, without remark. After a little I nerved myself up to my unpalatable job, and took the plunder back, crawling as before. It seemed the peculiarly appropriate attitude for the business I was in.

I was most honestly glad when it was over and done with.

About noon the next day Rayburn came, as usual, to report. I cut him short. I said, "Let this nonsense be dropped. We are making a bugaboo out of a poor little cub who has got no more harm in him than a hymn-book."

The sergeant looked surprised and said, "Well, you know it was your orders, sir, and I've got some of the writin'."

"And what does it amount to? How did you get it?"

"I peeped through the keyhole, and saw him writin'. So, when I judged he was about done, I made sort of a little cough, and I saw him crumple it up and throw it in the fire, and look all around to see if anybody was comin'. Then he settled back as comfortable and careless as anything. Then I comes in, and passes the time of day pleasantly, and sends him on an errand. He never looked uneasy, but went right along. It was a coal fire and new built; the writin' had gone over behind a chunk, out of sight; but I got it out; there it is; it ain't hardly scorched."

I glanced at the paper. Then I dismissed the sergeant and told him to send Webb to me. Here is the paper in full:

FORT TRUMBULL, the 8th. COLONEL

I was mistaken as to the caliber of the three guns I ended my list with. They are 18-pounders; all the rest of the armament is as I stated. The garrison remains as before reported, except that the two light infantry companies that were to be detached for service at the front are to stay here for the present—can't find out for how long, just now, but will soon. We are satisfied that, all things considered, matters had better be postponed un—

There it broke off—there is where Rayburn coughed and interrupted the writer. All my affection for the boy, all my respect for him and charity for his forlorn condition, withered in a moment under the blight of this cold-blooded baseness.

But never mind about that. Here was business that required profound and immediate attention. Webb and I turned the subject over and over, and examined it all around.

Webb said, "What a pity he was interrupted! Something is going to be postponed until—when? And what is the something? He would have mentioned it, the pious little reptile!"

"Yes," I said, "we have missed a trick. And who is 'we' in the letter? Is it conspirators inside the fort or outside?"

That "we" was uncomfortably suggestive. It was not worth guessing around, so we proceeded to matters more practical. First, we decided to double the sentries. Next, we decided we must have some more of the writings; so we began to plan to that end. And now we had an idea: Wicklow never went to the post-office—perhaps the deserted stable *was* his post-office. We sent for my confidential clerk—a young German named Sterne, who was a sort of natural detective—and told him all about the case. Within the hour we got word that Wicklow was writing again. Shortly afterward he had asked leave to go out into the town. He was detained awhile and meantime Sterne hurried off and concealed himself in the stable. By and by he saw Wicklow saunter in, look about him, then hide something under some rubbish in a corner, and take leisurely leave again. Sterne pounced upon the hidden article—a letter:

We think it best to postpone till the two companies are gone. I mean the four inside think so; I have yet to communicate with the others—afraid of attracting attention. I say four because we have lost two; they had hardly enlisted and got inside when they were shipped off to the front. It will be necessary to have two in their places. The two that went were the brothers from Thirty-mile Point. I have something of the greatest importance to reveal, but must not trust it to this method of communication; will try the other.

"The scoundrel!" said Webb. "Who could've supposed he was a spy? However, never mind about that; let us see how the case stands to date. First, we've got a rebel spy in our midst, whom we know. Second, we've got three more in our midst whom we don't know. Third, these spies have been introduced among us through the simple and easy process of enlisting as soldiers in the Union army—and evidently two of them have got sold at it, and been shipped off to the front; fourth, there are assistant spies 'outside'—number indefinite. And fifth, Wicklow has a very important matter which he is afraid to communicate by the 'present method'—will 'try the other.' That is the case, as it now stands. Shall we collar Wicklow and make him confess? Or shall we catch the person who removes the letters from the stable and make him tell? Or shall we keep still and find out more?"

We decided upon the last course. We judged that we did not need to proceed to summary measures now, since it was evident that the conspirators were likely to wait till those two infantry companies were out of the way. We fortified Sterne with ample powers, and told him to use his best endeavors to find out Wicklow's "other method" of communication. We meant to play a bold game; and to this end we proposed to keep the spies in an unsuspecting state as long as possible. So we ordered Sterne to return to the stable immediately, and, if he found the coast clear, to conceal Wicklow's letter where it was before, and leave it for the conspirators to get.

The night closed down without further event. It was cold and sleety, with a raw wind blowing; still I got out of my warm bed several times during the night, and did the rounds in person, to see that all was right and every sentry was on the alert. I always found them wide awake and watchful; evidently whispers of mysterious dangers had been floating about, and the doubling of the guards had been a kind of endorsement of these rumors. Once, toward morning, I encountered Webb, breasting his way against the bitter wind, and I learned that he, also, had been the rounds several times to see that all was going right.

Next day's events hurried things up somewhat. Wicklow wrote another letter, Sterne preceded him to the stable and saw him deposit it; captured it as soon as Wicklow was out of the way, then slipped out and followed the little spy at a distance, with a detective in plain clothes at his own heels, for we thought it judicious to have the law's assistance handy in case of need. Wicklow went to the railway station, and waited around till the train from New York came in, then stood scanning the faces of the crowd as they poured out of the cars. Presently an aged gentleman, with green goggles and a cane, came limping along, stopped in Wicklow's neighborhood, and began to look about him expectantly. In an instant Wicklow darted forward, thrust an envelope into his hand, then disappeared in the throng. The next instant Sterne had snatched the letter; and as he hurried past the detective, he said, "Follow the old gentleman—don't lose sight of him." Then Sterne scurried out with the crowd, and came straight to the fort.

First we opened the letter captured at the stable. It read:

HOLY ALLIANCE Found, in the usual gun, commands from the Master, left there last night, which set aside the instructions heretofore received from the subordinate quarter. Have left in the gun the usual indication that the commands reached the proper hand–

"Isn't the boy under constant surveillance?" Webb asked.

I said yes; he had been under strict surveillance ever since the capturing of his former letter.

"Then how could he put anything into a gun, or take anything out of it, and not get caught?"

"Well," I said, "I don't like the look of that very well."

"It means that there are conspirators among the sentinels," said Webb.

I sent for Rayburn, ordered him to examine the batteries, then the reading of the letter resumed:

> The new commands are peremptory, and require that the MMMM shall be FFFFF at 3 o'clock tomorrow morning. Two hundred will arrive, in small parties, by train and other means, from various directions, and will be at appointed place at right time. I will distribute the sign today. Success is apparently sure, though something must have got out, for the sentries have been doubled, and the chief went the rounds last night several times. W.W. comes from southerly today and will receive secret orders—by the other method. All six of you must be in 166 at sharp 2 a.m. You will find B.B. there, who will give you detailed instructions. Password same as last time, only revised—put first syllable last and last syllable first. REMEMBER XXXX. Do not forget. Be of good heart; before the next sun rises you will be heroes; your fame will be permanent; you will have added a deathless page to history. Amen.

"Thunder and Mars," said Webb, "but we are getting into mighty hot quarters, as I look at it!"

There was no question but that things were beginning to wear a most serious aspect. Said I, "A desperate enterprise is on foot; that is plain enough. Tonight is the time set for it—that, also, is plain. The exact nature of the enterprise—I mean the manner of it—is hidden away under those blind bunches of M's and F's, but the end and aim, I judge, is the surprise and capture of the post. We must move quick and sharp now. I think nothing can be gained by continuing our clandestine policy as regards Wicklow. We must know, and as soon as possible, where '166' is located, so that we can make a descent upon the gang there at 2:00 A.M.; and doubtless the quickest way to get that information will be to force it out of that boy. But before we make any important move, I must lay the facts before the War Department, and ask for plenary powers."

The despatch was prepared in cipher to go over the wires; I read it, approved it, and sent it along.

We presently finished discussing the letter which was under consideration, and then opened the one which had been snatched from the lame gentleman. It contained nothing but a couple of perfectly blank sheets of note-paper! It was a chilly check to our hot eagerness and expectancy. We felt as blank as the paper, for a moment, and twice as foolish. But it was for a moment only; for, of course, we immediately afterward thought of "sympathetic ink." We held the paper close to the fire and watched for the characters to come out, under the influence of the heat; but nothing appeared but some faint tracings, which we could make nothing of.

We then called in the surgeon, and sent him off with orders to apply every test he was acquainted with till he got the right one, and report the contents of the letter to me the instant he brought them to the surface. This check was a confounded annoyance, and we naturally chafed under the delay; for we had fully expected to get out of that letter some of the important secrets of the plot.

Now appeared Sergeant Rayburn, and drew from his pocket a piece of twine about a foot long, with three knots tied in it.

"I took the tompions out of all the guns and examined them closely," he said. "This string was the only thing that was in any gun."

So this bit of string was Wicklow's "sign" to signify that the "Master's" commands had not miscarried. I ordered that every sentinel who had served near that gun during the past twenty-four hours be put in confinement at once and separately, and not allowed to communicate with any one without my consent.

A telegram now came from the Secretary of War. It read:

Suspend Habeas Corpus. Put town under Martial Law. Make Necessary Arrests. Act with Vigor and Promptness. Keep the Department Informed.

We were now in shape to go to work. I had the lame gentleman quietly arrested and brought into the fort. I placed him under guard, and forbade speech to him or from him. He was inclined to bluster at first, but he soon dropped that.

Next came word that Wicklow had been seen to give something to a couple of our new recruits; and that, as soon as his back was turned, these had been seized and confined. Upon each was found a small bit of paper, bearing these words:

Eagles Third Flight
Remember XXXX—166

In accordance with instructions, I telegraphed the Department, in cipher, the progress made, and also described the above ticket. We seemed to be in a strong enough position now to throw off the mask as regarded Wicklow; so I sent for him. I also sent for and received back the letter written in sympathetic ink, the surgeon accompanying the letter with the information that thus far it had resisted his tests, but that there were others he could apply when I should be ready for him to do so.

Presently Wicklow entered. He had a somewhat worn and anxious look, but he was composed and easy, and if he suspected anything it did not appear in his face or manner. I allowed him to stand there a moment or two; then I said, "My boy, why do you go to that old stable so much?"

He answered, with simple demeanor and without embarrassment, "Well, I hardly know, sir; there isn't any particular reason, except that I like to be alone, and I amuse myself there."

"You amuse yourself there, do you?"

"Yes, sir," he replied, as innocently and simply as before.

"Is that all you do there?"

"Yes, sir," he said, looking up with childlike wonderment in his big, soft eyes.

"You are sure?"

"Yes, sir, sure."

After a pause, I asked, "why do you write so much?"

"I? I do not write much, sir."

"You don't?"

"No, sir. Oh, if you mean scribbling, I do scribble some, for amusement."

"What do you do with your scribblings?"

"Nothing, sir—throw them away."

"Never send them to anybody?"

"No, sir."

I suddenly thrust before him the letter to the "Colonel." He started slightly, but immediately composed himself. A slight tinge spread itself over his cheek.

"How came you to send this piece of scribbling, then?"

"I nev—never meant any harm, sir!"

"Never meant any harm! You betray the armament and condition of the post, and mean no harm by it?"

He hung his head and was silent.

"Come, speak up, and stop lying. Whom was this letter intended for?"

He showed signs of distress now; but quickly collected himself, and replied, in a tone of deep earnestness, "I will tell you the truth, sir—the whole truth. The letter was never intended for anybody at all. I wrote it only to amuse myself. I see the error and foolishness of it now; but it is the only offense, sir, upon my honor."

"Ah, I am glad of that. It is dangerous to be writing such letters. I hope you are sure this is the only one you wrote?"

"Yes, sir, perfectly sure." His hardihood was stupefying. He told that lie with as sincere a countenance as any creature ever wore.

I waited a moment to soothe down my rising temper, and then said, "Wicklow, jog your memory now, and see if you can help me with two or three little matters."

"I will do my very best, sir."

"Then, to begin with—who is 'the Master'?"

It betrayed him into darting a startled glance at our faces, but that was all. He was serene again in a moment, and tranquilly answered, "I do not know, sir."

"You are sure you do not know?"

He tried hard to keep his eyes on mine, but the strain was too great. His chin sunk toward his breast, and he stood there nervously fumbling with a button, an object to command one's pity, in spite of his base acts. Presently I broke the stillness with the question, "Who are the Holy Alliance?"

His body shook, and he made a slight random gesture with his hands, which to me was like the appeal of a despairing creature for compassion. But he made no sound. He continued to stand with his face bent toward the ground. As we sat gazing at him, waiting for him to speak, we saw the big tears begin to roll down his cheeks. But he remained silent. After a little, I said, "You must answer me, my boy, and you must tell me the truth. Who are the Holy Alliance?"

He wept on in silence. Presently I said, somewhat sharply, "Answer the question!"

He struggled to get command of his voice; then, looking up appealingly, forced the words out between his sobs, "Have pity on me, sir! I cannot answer it, for I do not know."

"What!"

"I am telling the truth. I never have heard of the Holy Alliance till this moment. On my honor, sir, this is so."

"Good heavens! Look at this second letter of yours. Do you see those words, 'Holy Alliance'? What do you say now?"

He gazed up into my face with the hurt look of one upon whom a great wrong had been wrought, then said, feelingly, "This is some cruel joke, sir; and how could they play it upon me, who have tried all I could to do right, and have never done harm to anybody? Some one has counterfeited my hand; I never wrote a line of this; I have never seen this letter before!"

"Oh, you unspeakable liar! Here, what do you say to this?"—and I snatched the sympathetic-ink letter from my pocket and thrust it before his eyes.

His face turned white—as white as a dead person's. He wavered slightly in his tracks, and put his hand against the wall to steady himself. After a moment he asked, in so faint a voice that it was hardly audible, "Have you—read it?"

Our faces must have answered the truth before my lips could get out a false "yes," for I distinctly saw the courage come back into that boy's eyes. I waited for him to say something, but he kept silent. So at last I said, "Well, what have you to say as to the revelations in this letter?"

He answered with perfect composure, "Nothing, except they're entirely harmless and innocent; they can hurt nobody."

I was in something of a corner now, as I couldn't disprove his assertion. I did not know exactly how to proceed. However, an idea came to my relief, and I said, "You are sure you know nothing about the Master and the Holy Alliance, and did not write the letter which you say is a forgery?"

"Yes, sir—sure."

I slowly drew out the knotted twine string and held it up without speaking. He gazed at it indifferently, then looked at me inquiringly. My patience was sorely taxed. However, I kept my temper down, and said, in my usual voice, "Wicklow, do you see this?"

"Yes, sir."

"What is it?"

"It seems to be a piece of string."

"Seems? It is a piece of string. Do you recognize it?"

"No, sir," he replied, as calmly as could be.

His coolness was wonderful! I paused now for several seconds, in order that the silence might add impressiveness to what I was about to say; then I rose and laid my hand on his shoulder, and said, gravely, "It will do you no good, poor boy, none in the world. This sign to the 'Master,' this knotted string, found in one of the guns on the—"

"Oh, no, no, no! Do not say in the gun, but in a crack in the tompion! It must have been in the crack!" And down he went on his knees and clasped his hands and lifted up a face that was pitiful to see, so ashy it was, and wild with terror.

"No, it was in the gun."

"Oh, something has gone wrong! My God, I am lost!" He sprang up and darted this way and that, dodging the hands that were put out to catch him, and doing his best to escape from the place.

But of course escape was impossible. Then he flung himself on his knees again, crying with all his might, and clasped me around the legs; and so he clung to me and begged and pleaded, saying, "Oh, have pity on me! Oh, be merciful to me! Protect me, save me. I will confess everything!"

It took us some time to quiet him down and modify his fright, and get him into something like a rational frame of mind. Then I began to question him, he answering humbly, with downcast eyes, and from time to time swabbing away his constantly flowing tears:

"So you are at heart a rebel?"

"Yes, sir."

"And a spy?"

"Yes, sir."

"Have been acting under distinct orders from outside?"

"Yes, sir."

"Willingly?"

"Yes, sir."

"Gladly, perhaps?"

"Yes, sir; it would do no good to deny it. The South is my country; my heart is Southern, and it is all in her cause."

"Then the tale you told me of the persecution of your family was made up for the occasion?"

"They—they told me to say it, sir."

"And you would betray and destroy those who pitied and sheltered you. Do you comprehend how base you are, you poor misguided thing?"

He replied with sobs only.

"Well, let that pass. To business. Who is the 'Colonel,' and where is he?"

He began to cry hard, and tried to beg off from answering. He said he would be killed if he told. I threatened to put him in the dark cell and lock him up if he did not come out with the information. At the same time I promised to protect him from all harm if he made a clean breast. For all answer, he closed his mouth firmly and put on a stubborn air which I could not bring him out of. At last I started with him; but a single glance into the dark cell converted him. He broke into a passion of weeping, and declared he would tell everything.

So I brought him back, and he named the "Colonel," and described him particularly. Said he would be found at the principal hotel in the town, in citizen's dress. I had to threaten him again, before he would describe and name the "Master." Said the Master would be found at No. 15 Bond Street, New York, passing under the name of R.F. Gaylord. I telegraphed name and description to the chief of police of the metropolis, and asked that Gaylord be arrested till I could send for him.

"Now," said I, "it seems that there are several of these conspirators 'outside,' presumably in New London. Name and describe them."

He named and described three men and two women—all stopping at the principal hotel. I sent out quietly, and had them and the "Colonel" arrested and confined in the fort.

"Next, I want to know all about your three fellow-conspirators who are here in the fort."

He was about to dodge me with a falsehood, I thought, but I produced the mysterious bits of paper which had been found upon two of them, and this had a salutary effect upon him. I said we had possession of two of the men, and he must point out the third.

This frightened him badly, and he cried out, "Oh, please don't make me; he would kill me on the spot!"

I said that that was all nonsense; I would have somebody near by to protect him. Besides, the men should be assembled without arms. I ordered all the raw recruits to be mustered, and then the poor, trembling little wretch went out and stepped along down the line, trying to look as indifferent as possible. Finally he spoke a single word to one of the men, and before he had gone five steps the man was under arrest.

As soon as Wicklow was with us again, I had those three men brought in. I made one of them stand forward, and said, "Now, Wicklow, mind, not a shade's divergence from the exact truth. Who is this man, and what do you know about him?"

Being "in for it," he cast consequences aside, fastened his eyes on the man's face, and spoke without hesitation. "His real name is George Bristow. He is from New Orleans; was second mate of the coast-packet Capitol two years ago; is a desperate character, and has served two terms for manslaughter—one for killing a deck-hand named Hyde with a capstan-bar, and one for killing a roustabout for refusing to heave the lead, which is no part of a roustabout's business. He is a spy, and was sent here by the Colonel to act in that capacity. He was third mate of the St. Nicholas when she blew up in the neighborhood of Memphis, in '58, and came near being lynched for robbing the dead and wounded while they were being taken ashore in an empty wood-boat."

And so forth and so on—he gave the man's biography in full. When he had finished, I said to the man, "What have you to say to this?"

"Barring your presence, sir, it is the infernalist lie that ever was spoke!"

I sent him back into confinement, and called the others forward in turn. Same result. The boy gave a detailed history of each, without ever hesitating. But all I could get out of either rascal was the indignant assertion that it was all a lie. They would confess nothing. I returned them to captivity, and brought out the rest of my prisoners, one by one. Wicklow told all about them—what towns in the South they were from, and every detail of their connection with the conspiracy.

But they all denied his facts, and not one of them confessed a thing. The men raged, the women cried. According to their stories, they were all innocent people from out West, and loved the Union above all things in this world. I locked the gang up, in disgust, and fell to catechizing Wicklow once more.

"Where is No. 166 and who is B.B.?"

Neither coaxing nor threats had any effect upon him. Time was flying—it was necessary to institute sharp measures. So I tied him up a-tiptoe by the thumbs. As the pain increased, it wrung screams from him which were almost more than I could bear. But I held my ground, and pretty soon he shrieked out, "Oh, please let me down, and I will tell!"

"No—you'll tell before I let you down."

Every instant was agony to him now, so out it came. "No. 166, Eagle Hotel!"—naming a wretched tavern down by the water, a resort of common laborers and less reputable folk.

So I released him, and then demanded to know the object of the conspiracy.

"To take the fort tonight," said he, doggedly and sobbing.

"Have I got all the chiefs of the conspiracy?"

"No. You've got all except those that are to meet at 166."

"What does 'Remember XXXX' mean?"

No reply.

"What is the password to No. 166?"

No reply.

"What do those bunches of letters mean—'FFFFF' and 'MMMM'? Answer! Or you will catch it again."

"I never will answer! I will die first."

"Think what you are saying, Wicklow. Is it final?"

He answered without a quiver in his voice, "It is. As sure as I love my wronged country and hate everything this Northern sun shines on, I will die before I will reveal those things."

I tied him up by the thumbs again. When the agony was full upon him it was heartbreaking to hear the poor thing's shrieks, but we got nothing else out of him. To every question he screamed the same reply, "I will die; but I will never tell."

We had to give it up. We were convinced that he would rather die than confess. So we took him down, and imprisoned him under strict guard. Then for some hours we busied ourselves with sending telegrams to the War Department, and with making preparations for a descent upon No. 166.

It was stirring times, that black and bitter night. Things had leaked out, and the whole garrison was on the alert. The sentinels were trebled, and nobody could move, outside or in, without being brought to a stand with a musket leveled at his head. However, Webb and I were less concerned now than we had previously been, because of the fact that the conspiracy must necessarily be in a pretty crippled condition, since so many of its principals were in our clutches.

I determined to be at No. 166 in good season, capture and gag B.B., and be on hand for the rest when they arrived. At about a quarter past one in the morning I crept out of the fortress with half a dozen stalwart and gamy U.S. regulars at my heels, and the boy Wicklow, with his hands tied behind him. I told him that we were going to No. 166, and that if I found he had lied again and was misleading us, he would have to show us the right place or suffer the consequences.

We approached the tavern stealthily and reconnoitered. A light was burning in the small barroom, the rest of the house was dark. I tried the front door; it yielded, and we softly entered, closing the door behind us. Then we removed our shoes, and I led the way to the barroom. The German landlord sat there, asleep in his chair. I woke him gently, and told him to take off his boots and precede us, warning him at the same time to utter no sound.

He obeyed without a murmur, but evidently he was badly frightened. I ordered him to lead the way to 166. We went up three flights of stairs as softly as a file of cats; and then, having arrived near the farther end of a long hall, we came to a door through the glazed transom of which we could discern the glow of a dim light from within. The landlord felt for me in the dark and whispered to me that this was 166. I tried the door—it was locked on the inside. I whispered an order to one of my biggest soldiers; we set our ample shoulders to the door, and with one heave we burst it from its hinges. I caught a half-glimpse of a figure in a bed—saw its head dart toward the candle; out went the light and we were in pitch darkness.

With one big bound I lit on that bed and pinned its occupant down with my knees. My prisoner struggled fiercely, but I got a grip on his throat with my left hand, and that was a good assistance to my knees in holding him down. Then straightway I snatched out my revolver, cocked it, and laid the cold barrel warningly against his cheek.

"Now somebody strike a light!" said I. "I've got him safe."

It was done. The flame of the match burst up. I looked at my captive, and, by George, it was a young woman!

I let go and got off the bed, feeling pretty sheepish. Everybody stared stupidly at his neighbor. Nobody had any wit or sense left, so sudden and overwhelming had been the surprise. The young woman began to cry, and covered her face with the sheet. The landlord said, meekly, "My daughter, she has been doing something that is not right?"

"Your daughter? Is she your daughter?"

"Oh yes, she is my daughter. She is just tonight come home from Cincinnati a little bit sick."

"Confound it, that boy has lied again. This is not the right 166; this is not B.B. Now, Wicklow, you will find the correct 166 for us, or—hello! Where is that boy?"

Gone, as sure as guns! And, what is more, we failed to find a trace of him. Here was an awful predicament. I cursed my stupidity in not tying him to one of the men; but it was of no use to bother about that now. What should I do in the present circumstances?—that was the question. That girl might be B.B., after all. I did not believe it, but still it would not answer to take unbelief for proof. So I finally put my men in a vacant room across the hall from 166, and told them to capture any-body that approached the girl's room, and to keep the landlord with them, and under strict watch, until further orders. Then I hurried back to the fort to see if all was right there yet.

Yes, all was right. And all remained right. I stayed up all night to make sure of that and was unspeakably glad to see the dawn come again, and be able to telegraph the Department that the Stars and Stripes still floated over Fort Trumbull.

An immense pressure was lifted from my breast. Still I did not relax vigilance either; the case was too grave for that. I had up my prisoners, one by one, and harried them by the hour, trying to get them to confess, but it was a failure. They only gnashed their teeth and tore their hair, and revealed nothing.

About noon came tidings of my missing boy. He had been seen on the road, tramping westward, some eight miles out, at six in the morning. I started a cavalry lieutenant and a private on his trail at once. They came in sight of him twenty miles out. He had climbed a fence and was wearily dragging himself across a slushy field toward a large old-fashioned mansion in the edge of a village. They rode through a bit of woods, made a detour, and closed upon the house from the opposite side; then dismounted and scurried into the kitchen. Nobody there. They slipped into the next room, which was also unoccupied; the door from that room into the front or sitting room was open. They were about to step through it when they heard a low voice; it was somebody praying. So they halted reverently, and the lieutenant put his head in and saw an old man and an old woman kneeling in a corner of that sitting-room. It was the old man that was praying, and just as he was finishing his prayer, the Wicklow boy opened the front door and stepped in. Both of those old people sprang at him and smothered him with embraces, shouting, "Our boy! Our darling! God be praised. The lost is found! He that was dead is alive again!"

Well, sir, what do you think! That young imp was born and reared on that homestead, and had never been five miles away from it in all his life till the fortnight before he loafed into my quarters and gulled me with that maudlin yarn of his!

It's as true as gospel. That old man was his father—a learned old retired clergyman, and that old lady was his mother.

Let me throw in a word or two of explanation concerning that boy and his performances. It turned out that he was a ravenous devourer of dime novels and sensation-story papers—therefore, dark mysteries and gaudy heroisms were just in his line. Then he had read newspaper reports of the stealthy goings and comings of rebel spies in our midst, and of their lurid purposes and their two or three startling achieve-ments, till his imagination was all aflame on that subject. His constant comrade for some months had been a Yankee youth of much tongue and lively fancy, who had served for a couple years as "mud clerk" (that is, subordinate purser) on certain of the packet-boats plying between New Orleans and points two or three hundred miles up the Mississippi—hence his easy facility in handling the names and other details pertaining to that region.

Now I had spent two or three months in that part of the country before the war; and I knew just enough about it to be easily taken in by that boy, whereas a born Louisianian would probably have caught him tripping before he had talked fifteen minutes. Do you know the reason he said he would rather die than explain certain of his treasonable enigmas? Simply because he couldn't explain them! They had no meaning. He had fired them out of his imagination without forethought or afterthought; and so, upon sudden call, he wasn't able to invent an explanation of them.

For instance, he could not reveal what was hidden in the "sympathetic ink" letter, for there wasn't anything hidden in it—it was blank paper only. He hadn't put anything into a gun, and had never intended to—for his letters were all written to imaginary persons, and when he hid one in the stable he always removed the one he had put there the day before; so he was not acquainted with that knotted string, since he was seeing it for the first time when I showed it to him. But as soon as I had let him find out where it came from, he straightway adopted it, in his romantic fashion, and got some fine effects out of it. He invented Mr. "Gaylord"; there wasn't any 15 Bond Street, just then—it had been pulled down three months before.

He invented the "Colonel"; he invented the glib histories of those unfortunate ones whom I captured and confronted him with; he invented "B.B."; he even invented No. 166, one might say, for he didn't know there was such a number in the Eagle Hotel until we went there. He stood ready to invent anybody or anything whenever it was wanted. If I called for "outside" spies, he promptly described strangers whom he had seen at the hotel, and whose names he had happened to hear. Ah, he lived in a gorgeous, romantic, mysterious world during those few stirring days, and I think it was real to him, and that he enjoyed it clear down to the bottom of his heart.

But he made trouble enough for us, and just no end of humiliation. You see, on account of him we had fifteen or twenty people under arrest and confinement in the fort, with sentinels before their doors. A lot of the captives were soldiers and such, and to them I didn't have to apologize; but the rest were first-class citizens, from all over the country, and no amount of apologies was sufficient to satisfy them. They just fumed and raged and made no end of trouble! And those two ladies—one was an Ohio Congressman's wife, the other a Western bishop's sister—well, the scorn and ridicule and angry tears they poured out on me made up a keepsake that was likely to make me remember them for a considerable time—and I shall. That old lame gentleman with the goggles was a college president from Philadelphia, who had come up to attend his nephew's funeral. He had never seen Wicklow before, of course. Well, he not only missed the funeral, and got jailed as a rebel spy, but Wicklow had stood up there in my quarters and coldly described him as a counterfeiter, horse-thief, and firebug from the most notorious rascal-nest in Galveston; and this was a thing which that poor gentleman couldn't seem to get over at all.

And the War Department! But, oh, my soul, let's draw the curtain over that part!

THE OBLONG BOX
by Edgar Allan Poe

Known primarily as a horror writer, Edgar Allan Poe is considered to be a master of the mystery genre as well. With over seventy works of short fiction ranging from the grotesque to the demented, the infamous writer, born in Boston on January 19, 1809, led a childhood as unusual as his writings.

Abandoned by his actor father shortly after his birth, and losing his actress mother to an early death when he was only three, Poe was separated from his brother and sister when he was taken in by a rich tobacco merchant named John Allan. Moving to Virginia with Allan, Poe was then educated in private academies, and though he did very well in school, he was still excluded from the Virginia elite because he was the child of actors.

In 1826, he entered the University of Virginia, and not only got himself dismissed from that institution for gambling, but later was also expelled from West Point for lack of attendance. Enraged, John Allan refused to pay Poe's considerable debts and never forgave him for dishonoring his family name.

After these crises, Poe moved back to Boston and enlisted in the army under the name of Edgar A. Perry. It was in Boston that Poe was discovered by a printer who published his first book, Tamerlane and Other Poems, in 1827. Ironically, his name, which one day would be known around the world, did not appear on the title page, and the book was simply said to be "By a Bostonian."

From that time on, Poe wrote rather prolifically, though few of his works brought him success. In 1831, Poe decided to live with his grandmother, Maria Poe, his cousin, Virginia Clemm, and her mother, Maria Clemm. And on May 16, Poe married Virginia, who was only thirteen years old. After Poe's grandmother died in 1835, the couple lived happily with Virginia's mother for many years.

But in 1842, Virginia Poe suffered her first attack of tuberculosis, and Poe agonized over his beloved wife's poor health until her death on January 30, 1847. Two years later, after his slow emotional recovery from Virginia's death, Poe was traveling from Richmond to New York to fetch Maria Clemm. He stopped in Baltimore on the way to attend a friend's birthday party, where it is said he drank until he collapsed. Several days later, on election day, October 3, he was discovered to be severely ill and delirious outside a polling place. Five days later, on October 7, 1849, he died, many say due to alcoholism.

Best known for his extraordinary works such as "The Raven," "The Tell-tale Heart," and "The Cask of Amontillado," Poe's unique gift of blending irony with horror emerges in nearly all of his works. In "The Oblong Box," the narrator discovers that his friend Mr. Wyatt has boarded the same ship that he has. However, for some odd reason, Mr. Wyatt has rented an extra compartment, in which he keeps a mysterious-looking, oblong box. The narrator is obsessed with that box . . . are you?

Some years ago, I engaged passage from Charleston, S.C., to New York, in the fine ship "Independence." We were to sail on the fifteenth of the month (June), weather permitting; and, on the fourteenth, I went on board to arrange some matters in my stateroom.

I found that we were to have a great many passengers, including a more than usual number of ladies. On the list were several of my acquaintances; and among other names, I was rejoiced to see that of Mr. Cornelius Wyatt, a young artist, for whom I entertained feelings of warm friendship. He had been with me a fellow student at C—University, where we were very much together. He had the ordinary temperament of genius, and was a compound of misanthropy, sensibility, and enthusiasm. To these qualities he united the warmest and truest heart which ever beat in a human bosom.

I observed that his name was carded upon three staterooms; and, upon again referring to the list of passengers, I found that he had engaged passage for himself, wife, and two sisters—his own. The staterooms were sufficiently roomy, and each had two berths, one above the other. These berths were so exceedingly narrow as to be insufficient for more than one person; still I could not comprehend why there were three staterooms for these four persons. I was, just at that epoch, in one of those moody frames of mind which make a man abnormally inquisitive about trifles; and I confess with shame that I busied myself in a variety of ill-bred and preposterous conjectures about this matter of the supernumerary stateroom. It was no business of mine, to be sure, but with nonetheless pertinacity did I occupy myself in attempts to resolve the enigma. At last I reached a conclusion which wrought in me great wonder why I had not arrived at it before.

"It is a servant, of course," I said. "What a fool I am, not sooner to have thought of so obvious a solution!" And then I again repaired to the list—but here I saw distinctly that no servant was to come with the party—although, in fact, it had been the original design to bring one—the words "and servant" had been first written and then overscored. "Oh, extra baggage, to be sure," I now said to myself—"something he wishes not to be put in the hold—something to be kept under his own eye—ah, I have it—a painting or so—this is what he has been bargaining about with Nicolino, the Italian." This idea satisfied me, and I dismissed my curiosity for the nonce.

Wyatt's two sisters I knew very well, and most amiable and clever girls they were. His wife he had newly married, and I had never yet seen her. He had often talked about her, however, and in his usual style of enthusiasm. He described her as of surpassing beauty, wit, and accomplishment, and I was quite anxious to make her acquaintance.

On the day I visited the ship (the fourteenth), Wyatt and party were also to visit it—so the captain informed me—and I waited on board an hour longer than I had designed, in hope of being presented to the bride; but then an apology came. "Mrs. W. was a little indisposed, and would decline coming on board until tomorrow, at the hour of sailing."

The morrow having arrived, I was going from my hotel to the wharf, when Captain Hardy met me and said that, "owing to circumstances" (a stupid but convenient phrase), "he rather thought the 'Independence' would not sail for a day or two, and that when all was ready, he would send up and let me know." This I thought strange, for there was a stiff southerly breeze; but as "the circumstances" were not forthcoming, although I pumped for them with much perseverance, I had nothing to do but to return home and digest my impatience at leisure.

I did not receive the expected message from the captain for nearly a week. It came at length, however, and I immediately went on board. The ship was crowded with passengers, and everything was in the bustle attendant upon making sail.

Wyatt's party arrived in about ten minutes after myself. There were the sisters, the bride, and the artist—the latter in one of his customary fits of moody misanthropy. I was too well used to these, however, to pay them any special attention. He didn't even introduce me to his wife; this courtesy devolving, per force, upon his sister Marian, a very sweet and intelligent girl who, in a few hurried words, made us acquainted.

Mrs. Wyatt had been closely veiled, and when she raised her veil in acknowledging my bow, I confess that I was very profoundly astonished. I should have been much more so, however, had not long experience advised me not to trust, with too implicit a reliance, the enthusiastic descriptions of my friend, the artist, when indulging in comments upon the loveliness of women. When beauty was the theme, I well knew with what facility he soared into the regions of the purely ideal.

The truth is, I could not help regarding Mrs. Wyatt as a decidedly plain-looking woman. If not positively ugly, she was not, I think, very far from it. She was dressed, however, in exquisite taste, and I had no doubt that she had captivated my friend's heart by the more enduring graces of the intellect and soul. She said very few words, and passed at once into her stateroom with Mr. W.

My inquisitiveness now returned. There was no servant —that was a settled point. I looked, therefore, for the extra baggage. After some delay, a cart arrived at the wharf, with an oblong pine box, which was everything that seemed to be expected. Immediately upon its arrival we made sail, and in a short time were safely over the bar and standing out to sea.

The box in question was, as I say, oblong. It was about six feet in length by two and a half in breadth; I observed it attentively, and like to be precise. Now this shape was peculiar, and no sooner had I seen it, than I took credit to myself for the accuracy of my guessing. I had reached the conclusion, it will be remembered, that the extra baggage of my friend, the artist, would prove to be pictures, or at least a picture; for I knew he had been for several weeks in conference with Nicolino:—and now here was a box, which, from its shape, could possibly contain nothing in the world but a copy of Leonardo's "Last Supper"; and a copy of this very "Last Supper," done by Rubini the younger, at Florence, I had known, for some time, to be in the possession of Nicolino. This point, therefore, I considered as sufficiently settled.

I chuckled excessively when I thought of my acumen. It was the first time I had ever known Wyatt to keep from me any of his artistical secrets; but here he evidently intended to steal a march upon me, and smuggle a fine picture to New York, under my very nose; expecting me to know nothing of the matter.

I resolved to quiz him well, now and hereafter.

One thing, however, annoyed me not a little. The box did not go into the extra stateroom. It was deposited in Wyatt's own; and there, too, it remained, occupying very nearly the whole of the floor—no doubt to the exceeding discomfort of the artist and his wife;—this the more especially as the tar or paint with which it was lettered in sprawling capitals, emitted a strong, disagreeable, and, to my fancy, a peculiarly disgusting odor. On the lid were painted the words—"Mrs. Adelaide Curtis, Albany, New York. Charge of Cornelius Wyatt, Esq. This side up. To be handled with care."

Now, I was aware that Mrs. Adelaide Curtis was the artist's wife's mother;—but then I looked upon the whole address as a mystification, intended especially for myself. I made up my mind, of course, that the box and contents would never get farther north than the studio of my misanthropic friend, in Chambers Street, New York.

For the first three or four days we had fine weather, although the wind was dead ahead; having chopped round to the northward, immediately upon our losing sight of the coast. The passengers were, consequently, in high spirits and dis-posed to be social. I must except, however, Wyatt and his two sisters, who behaved stiffly, and, I could not help thinking, uncourteously to the rest of the party.

Wyatt's conduct I did not so much regard. He was gloomy, even beyond his usual habit—in fact he was morose—but in him I was prepared for eccentricity. For the sisters, however, I could make no excuse. They secluded them-selves in their staterooms the greater part of the passage, and absolutely refused, although I repeatedly urged them, to hold communication with any person on board.

Mrs. Wyatt herself was far more agreeable. That is to say, she was chatty; and to be chatty is no slight recommendation at sea. She became excessively intimate with most of the ladies, and to my profound astonishment, evinced no equivocal dis-position to coquet with the men. She amused us all very much. I say "amused"—and scarcely know how to explain myself. The truth is, I soon found that Mrs. W. was far oftener laughed at than with. The gentlemen said little about her, but the ladies, in a little while, pronounced her "a good-hearted thing, rather indifferent-looking, totally uneducated, and decidedly vulgar." The great wonder was how Wyatt had been entrapped into such a match. Wealth was the general solu-tion—but this I knew to be no solution at all; for Wyatt had told me that she neither brought him a dollar nor had any expectations from any source whatever. "He had married," he said, "for love, and for love only, and his bride was far more than worthy of his love."

When I thought of these expressions on the part of my friend, I confess that I felt indescribably puzzled. Could it be possible that he was taking leave of his senses? What else could I think? He, so refined, so intellectual, so fastidious, with so exquisite a perception of the faulty and so keen an appreciation of the beautiful! To be sure, the lady seemed especially fond of him, particularly so in his absence, when she made herself ridiculous by frequent quotations of what had been said by her "beloved husband, Mr. Wyatt." The word "husband" seemed forever—to use one of her delicate expressions—"on the tip of her tongue." In the meantime, it was observed by all on board that he avoided her in the most pointed manner, and, for the most part, shut himself up alone in his stateroom, where he might have been said to live altogether, leaving his wife at full liberty to amuse herself as she thought best, in the public society of the main cabin.

My conclusion, from what I saw and heard, was that the artist, by some unaccountable freak of fate, or perhaps in some fit of enthusiastic and fanciful passion, had been induced to unite himself with a person altogether beneath him and that the natural result, entire and speedy disgust, had ensued. I pitied him from the bottom of my heart, but could not, for that reason, quite forgive his incommunicativeness in the matter of the "Last Supper." For this I resolved to have my revenge.

One day he came upon deck, and taking his arm as had been my wont, I sauntered with him backward and forward. His gloom, however (which I considered quite natural under the circumstances), seemed entirely unabated. He said little, and that moodily, and with evident effort. I ventured a jest, and he made a sickening attempt at a smile. Poor fellow!—as I thought of his wife, I wondered that he could have heart to put on even the semblance of mirth. At last I ventured a home thrust. I determined to commence a series of covert insinuations, or innuendoes, about the oblong box— just to let him perceive, gradually, that I was not altogether the victim of his little bit of pleasant mystification. My first observation was by way of opening a masked battery. I said something about the "peculiar shape of that box" and as I spoke the words, I smiled knowingly, winked, and touched him gently with my forefinger in the ribs.

The manner in which Wyatt received this harmless pleasantry convinced me, at once, that he was mad. He stared at me as if he found it impossible to comprehend the witticism of my remark; but as its point seemed slowly to make its way into his brain, his eyes, in the same proportion, seemed protruding from their sockets. Then he grew very red—then hideously pale—then, as if highly amused with what I had insinuated, he began a loud and boisterous laugh, which, to my astonishment, he kept up with gradually increasing vigor for ten minutes or more. In conclusion, he fell flat and heavily upon the deck.

When I ran to him, to all appearance he was dead. I called assistance, and with much difficulty we brought him to himself. Upon reviving, he spoke incoherently for some time. At length we bled him and put him to bed. The next morning he was recovered, so far as regarded his bodily health. Of his mind I say nothing, of course. I avoided him during the rest of the passage, by advice of the captain, who seemed to coincide with me in my views of his insanity, but cautioned me to say nothing about his head to any person on board.

Several circumstances occurred immediately after this fit of Wyatt's which contributed to heighten the curiosity with which I was already possessed. Among other things, this: I had been nervous—drank too much stong green tea, and slept ill at night—in fact, for two nights I could not be properly said to sleep at all. Now, my stateroom opened into the main cabin, or dining room, as did those of all the single men on board. Wyatt's three rooms were in the after cabin, separated from the main one by a sliding door, never locked even at night. As we were almost constantly on a wind, and the breeze was not a little stiff, the ship heeled to leeward very considerably; and whenever her starboard side was to leeward, the sliding door between the cabins slid open, and so remained, nobody taking the trouble to get up and shut it. But my berth was in such a position that when my own stateroom door was open, as well as the sliding door in question (and my own door was always open on account of the heat) I could see into the after cabin quite distinctly, and just at that portion of it, too, where were situated the staterooms of Mr. Wyatt.

Well, during two nights (not consecutive) while I lay awake, I clearly saw Mrs. W. about eleven o'clock upon each night, steal cautiously from the stateroom of Mr. W. and enter the extra room, where she remained until daybreak, when she was called by her husband and went back. That they were virtually separated was clear. They had separate apartments, no doubt in contemplation of a more permanent divorce; and here, after all, I thought was the mystery of the extra stateroom.

There was another circumstance, too, which interested me much. During the two wakeful nights in question, and immediately after the disappearance of Mrs. Wyatt into the extra stateroom, I was attracted by certain singular, cautious, subdued noises in that of her husband. After listening to them for some time with thoughtful attention, I at length succeeded in translating their import. They were sounds occasioned by the artist in prying open the oblong box by means of a chisel and mallet—the latter being apparently muffled, or deadened, by some soft woollen or cotton substance in which its head was enveloped.

In this manner I fancied I could distinguish the precise moment when he fairly disengaged the lid—also, that I could determine when he removed it altogether, and when he deposited it upon the lower berth in his room; this latter point I knew, for example, by certain slight taps which the lid made in striking against the wooden edges of the berth, as he endeavored to lay it down very gently, there being no room for it on the floor. After this there was a dead stillness, and I heard nothing more upon either occasion until nearly daybreak; unless, perhaps, I may mention a low sobbing or murmuring sound, so very much suppressed as to be nearly inaudible—if, indeed, the whole of this latter noise were not rather produced by my own imagination.

I say it seemed to resemble sobbing or sighing, but, of course, it could not have been either. I rather think it was a ringing in my own ears. Mr. Wyatt, no doubt, according to custom, was merely giving the rein to one of his hobbies—indulging in one of his fits of artistic enthusiasm. He had opened his oblong box in order to feast his eyes on the treasure within. There was nothing in this, however, to make him sob. I repeat, therefore, that it must have been simply a freak of my own fancy, distempered by good Captain Hardy's green tea. Just before dawn, on each of the two nights of which I speak, I distinctly heard Mr. Wyatt replace the lid upon the oblong box and force the nails into their old places by means of the muffled mallet. Having done this, he issued from his stateroom fully dressed, and proceeded to call Mrs. W. from hers.

We had been at sea seven days, and were now off Cape Hatteras, when there came a tremendously heavy blow from the southwest. We were prepared for it, however, as the weather had been holding out threats for some time. Everything was made snug, and as the wind steadily freshened, we lay to, under spanker and fore topsail, both double-reefed.

In this trim we rode safely enough for forty-eight hours— the ship proving herself an excellent sea-boat in many respects, and shipping no water of any consequence. At the end of this period, however, the gale had freshened into a hurricane, and our aftersail split into ribbons, bringing us so much in the trough of the water that we shipped several prodigious seas, one immediately after the other. By this accident we lost three men overboard with the caboose, and nearly the whole of the larboard bulwarks. Scarcely had we recovered our senses, before the fore topsail went into shreds, when we got up a storm staysail, and with this did pretty well for some hours, the ship heading the sea much more steadily than before.

The gale still held on , however, and we saw no signs of its abating. The rigging was found to be ill-fitted, and greatly strained; and on the third day of the blow, our mizzenmast, in a heavy lurch to windward, went by the board.

For an hour or more we tried in vain to get rid of it on account of the prodigious rolling of the ship, and before we had succeeded, the carpenter came aft and announced four feet of water in the hold. To add to our dilemma, we found the pumps choked and nearly useless.

All was now confusion and despair, but an effort was made to lighten the ship by throwing overboard as much of her cargo as could be reached, and by cutting away the two masts that remained. This we at last accomplished, but we were still unable to do anything at the pumps, and in the meantime, the leak gained on us very fast.

At sundown the gale had sensibly diminished in violence, and, as the sea went down with it, we still entertained faint hopes of saving ourselves in the boats. At eight P.M., the clouds broke away, and we had the advantage of a full moon—a piece of fortune which served to cheer our drooping spirits.

After incredible labor we succeeded, at length, in getting the longboat over the side without accident, and into this we crowded the whole of the crew and most of the passengers. This party made off immediately, and after undergoing much suffering, finally arrived in safety at Ocracoke Inlet, on the third day after the wreck.

Fourteen passengers, with the captain, remained on board, resolving to trust their fortunes to the jollyboat at the stem. We lowered it without difficulty, although it was only by a miracle that we prevented it from swamping as it touched the water. It contained, when afloat, the captain and his wife, Mr. Wyatt and party, a Mexican officer, wife, four children, and myself, with a valet.

We had no room, of course, for anything except necessary instruments, some provisions, and the clothes upon our backs. No one had thought of even attempting to save any-thing more. What must have been the astonishment of all then, when, having proceeded a few fathoms from the ship, Mr. Wyatt stood up in the stern sheets, and coolly demanded of Captain Hardy that the boat be put back for the purpose of taking in his oblong box!

"Sit down, Mr. Wyatt," replied the captain, somewhat sternly, "you will capsize us if you do not sit quite still. Our gunwale is almost in the water now."

"The box!" vociferated Mr. Wyatt, still standing—"the box I say! Captain Hardy, you cannot, you will not refuse me. Its weight will be but a trifle—it is nothing—mere nothing. By the mother who bore you for the love of Heaven, by your hope of salvation, I implore you to put back for the box!"

The captain, for a moment, seemed touched by the earnest appeal of the artist, but he regained his stern composure, and merely said:

"Mr. Wyatt, you are mad. I cannot listen to you. Sit down, I say, or you will swamp the boat. Stay—hold him—seize him!—he is about to spring overboard! There—I knew it—he is over!"

As the captain said this, Mr. Wyatt sprang from the boat, and, as we were yet in the lee of the wreck, succeeded by almost superhuman exertion, in getting hold of a rope which hung from the forechains. In another moment he was on board and rushing frantically down into the cabin.

In the meantime, we had been swept astern of the ship, and being quite out of her lee, were at the mercy of the tremendous sea which was still running. We made a determined effort to put back, but our little boat was like a feather in the breath of the tempest. We saw at a glance that the doom of the unfortunate artist was sealed.

As our distance from the wreck rapidly increased, the madman (for as such only could we regard him) was seen to emerge from the companionway, up which by dint of strength that appeared gigantic, he dragged, bodily, the oblong box. While we gazed in the extremity of astonishment, he passed rapidly several turns of a three-inch rope, first around the box and then around his body. In another instant both body and box were in the sea— disappearing suddenly, at once and forever.

We lingered awhile upon our oars, with our eyes riveted upon the spot. At length we pulled away. The silence remained unbroken for an hour. Finally, I hazarded a remark.

"Did you observe, captain, how suddenly they sank? Was not that an exceedingly singular thing? I confess that I entertained some feeble hope of his final deliverance when I saw him lash himself to the box and commit himself to the sea."

"They sank as a matter of course," replied the captain, "and that like a shot. They will soon rise again, however—but not till the salt melts."

"The salt!" I exclaimed.

"Hush!" said the captain, pointing to the wife and sisters of the deceased. "We must talk of these things at some more appropriate time."

We suffered much and made a narrow escape, but fortune befriended us and our mates in the longboat. We landed, more dead than alive, after four days of intense distress, upon the beach opposite Roanoke Island. We remained here a week, were not ill-treated by the wreckers, and at length obtained a passage to New York.

A month after the loss of the "Independence," I happened to meet Captain Hardy in Broadway. Our conversation turned, naturally, upon the disaster, and especially upon the sad fate of poor Wyatt. I thus learned the following particulars.

The artist had engaged passage for himself, wife, sisters, and a servant. His wife was, as she had been represented, a most lovely, and most accomplished woman. On the morning of the fourteenth of June (the day I first visited the ship), the lady suddenly sickened and died. The young husband was frantic with grief—but circumstances imperatively forbade the deferring of his voyage to New York. It was necessary to take to her mother the corpse of his adored wife, and on the other hand, the universal prejudice which would prevent his doing so openly was well known. Nine tenths of the passengers would have abandoned the ship rather than take passage with a dead body.

In this dilemma, Captain Hardy arranged that the corpse, being partially embalmed and packed with a large quantity of salt in a box of suitable dimensions, should be conveyed on board as merchandise. Nothing was to be said of the lady's decease, and as it was well understood that Mr. Wyatt had engaged passage for his wife, it became necessary that some person should personate her during the voyage. This the deceased lady's maid was easily prevailed on to do. The extra stateroom, originally engaged for this girl, during her mistress' life, was now retained. In this stateroom the pseudo-wife slept, of course, every night. In the daytime she performed, to the best of her ability, the part of her mistress—whose person, it had been carefully ascertained, was unknown to any of the passengers on board.

My own mistake arose, naturally enough, through too careless, too inquisitive, and too impulsive a temperament. But of late, it is a rare thing that I sleep soundly at night. There is a countenance which haunts me, turn as I will. And there is a hysterical laugh which will forever ring within my ears.

Glossary

aerated water—water filled with gas, creating bubbles

antecedent—going before; preceding

appropriated—to take possession of

benefactors—people who give a charitable donation

brougham—a closed carriage seating two or four persons

conscientious—having a sense of right and wrong

despondent—depressed; dejected

eccentric—odd; unusual; peculiar

exonerate—free from blame

extradited—to turn over to a different jurisdiction,
as a prisoner

fathom—a nautical unit of length, containing six feet

festoons—garlands hanging in a curve, used for decoration

garrison—a fortified place in which troops are quartered

impediment—hindrance; obstruction

imposing—impressive by appearance or manner

innuendo—a remote reference, especially one reflecting
discredit on another person

leeward—the side of a ship away from where the wind is
blowing

misanthropy—hating mankind

modulated—to vary the tone of, as in speaking or singing

reconnoitered—made a preliminary survey in preparation
for military operations

ruffian—a noisy, brutal, cruel person

tompion—a plug or cover for the muzzle of a gun

umbrage—resentment

unconscionable—having no conscience; unscrupulous

vociferated—cried out loudly

yawl—a ship's small boat